"Wil . . ."

His mother's voice was what Wil called Grownup-Serious.

"What, Mom?"

She held up the note he'd left that morning. "I just want to know a little more about this island. All of a sudden an island. Out of nowhere, an island. What does it mean?"

His father sat at the table, took a sip of coffee, and looked sharply at Wil. "What island?"

"This." His mother handed over the note. "Wil left it this morning. I just want to know about it. How come an island all of a sudden?"

Wil smiled. "It's not all of a sudden. I mentioned it the other night, but I guess you didn't hear me. It's just a small island in a lake up the road. Kind of a neat place. I've been there a couple of times now and sort of camp and look at things. It's not a big deal. . . ." But even as he said it, he knew that it was—in his mind it had become a big deal.

GARY PAULSEN has written many distinguished books for young readers, including *The Crossing*, available in a Laurel-Leaf edition. He lives in Leonard, Minnesota.

THE ISLAND

Gary Paulsen

LAUREL-LEAF BOOKS

ISBN: 0-440-20632-4

RL: 5.7

Reprinted by arrangements with Franklin Watts, Inc., on behalf of
Orchard Books

Printed in the United States of America

May 1990

15   14   13   12   11   10   9   8

OPM

This book is dedicated
with deep affection to
MIKE PRINTZ
for his great-hearted love of books
and the art of writing

THE island lay in almost the exact center of a small lake in northern Wisconsin, seven miles north of the town of Maypine, fifteen miles east of the town of Pinewood—both named after the pine forests that had once been prominent and were now logged off— and was thought so unimportant that it appeared on no topographical maps of the area.

Indians had named the lake after its principal fish, a rough bottom-feeder called the sucker. When white men came to put their name on it, they followed suit and called it Sucker Lake; and for that reason the lake had been spared the building and crowding that came to many lakes in the northern fishing regions. Fishermen bent on spending their vacations and money trying for lake trout or bass or muskies were decidedly shy about taking time to fish a lake named after a soft-flesh fish many considered fit only for fertilizer or pet food; and then too, suckers were normally associated with muddy lakes and dirty water—neither of which brought tourists. For that reason no resorts were built on the lake or anywhere nearby; and since the land around was rocky and had poor topsoil, no farmers settled there and the lake was left alone to exist much as it had since an Ice Age glacier had scooped it out and filled it.

Somehow the glacier, in its slow grind across the north, had missed a U-shaped spot in the middle of the lake and left a rise of land that became a rocky island. The left arm of the island was a sandy-dirt beach, from which the main body ran south, curved east and then back again to the north, making a small north-facing bay about a hundred yards across. Wild rice stalks lined the bay, and some tree snags rose out of the water— old hardwoods that had died and not yet rotted.

There were fewer than four inches of topsoil on the island, and no large trees could grow, only a handful of poplars about twenty-five feet high, some small jack-pine not over twenty feet, and a scattering of red willow and hazel brush, all of which covered only the main body of the island itself and did not extend up into the arms of the U. The rest of it was covered by timothy grass and tightly woven weeds and clover, up to waist height where the soil was thickest, down to nothing where the rock was exposed.

The shore of the island facing north was a rim of beach about ten feet wide; the outside or southern edge was made up largely of rocks, curved and rounded by the ageless chewing of small waves pushed by the fall wind before the freezeup. On the right arm of the U a flat rock, about twenty feet long, projected out into the water and made a platform or table. This rock was so square it seemed almost sculpted—although it had been broken naturally by the glacier along straight fault lines —and seemed somehow out of place because of its sharp corners and flawless edges.

It can only be guessed what had happened on and

to the island in the time before. Summer to winter to summer, over countless ages, it had been forming and changing. Once there had not been a lake, only a swamp and giant beasts that shook the ground when they passed the high point that became the island. Before, all was covered by sea, and fish as large as boats, huge sharks, swam hunting past the rocks that became the island. When the sea was gone, there came the ice, the great sheet of blue-white cold that covered all there was, and everything died or was made to sleep and wait for thousands of years. And when the ice was gone, it left a huge lake, a freshwater lake as large as many seas; and when that was gone, before man still, before we know of men or before there were men to know of men, the massive lake withdrew and left the smaller lakes. And from that time on it left the island.

From the time before, it is only possible to guess, only possible to dream of the battles of the dinosaurs tearing the earth and sharks as large as boats whipping ocean currents with their tails, only possible to imagine the saber-tooth tigers and mastodons and the men who could live with nothing but their minds as tools. From all of that time the small island in almost the exact center of Sucker Lake in the northern part of Wisconsin cannot be known, can only be part of theory and ideas. Hopes. Wishes. Dreams.

But in the summer of the middle of his fifteenth year on earth Wil Neuton discovered the island, or was discovered by the island—he was never sure which—and from that time on it is not necessary to guess about it any longer but only necessary to know Wil.

1.

Part of our problem is that we run around naming things with-out asking them if they want to be named. Then after we name them, they don't know they're named anyway. A tree doesn't know it's a tree; a fish doesn't know it's a fish; and if the fish did know, it would probably be upset by it. Who wants to be called fish?

—Wil Neuton

EVEN at fourteen, Wil Neuton towered over his parents. They were short, and somehow the genes had jumped a generation and made him tall—six feet, two inches—and had given him breadth, a strong body with wide shoulders and long legs and muscled arms with big hands. He was brown-blond, with brown eyes and some freckles across his nose and cheeks, the kind of freckles parents and aunts who visit once a year "just love" but which the owner of those freckles hates. When he was small, one visiting aunt, whose name was honestly Clara, would reach down and pinch his cheeks and say things that were supposed to be cute about the freckles. But when Wil grew taller, and taller still, Clara gave it up because she had to stand on tiptoe to get a good hold on his cheek, and even Clara, in her once-a-year wisdom, knew that it looked silly to be hanging on the cheek of somebody over six feet tall.

But the freckles were still there, as well as even, white teeth and a fast smile that made tight crinkles at the corners of his eyes. When Clara could no longer grab his freckled cheek, she settled on his teeth and smile. On her yearly visits she would insist, "Smile and show me your teeth. Come on, smile now."

The first Thursday after school let out for the summer, Wil's father caught both Wil and his mother at the same time in the kitchen before they could get away, and he began a conference. He loved to hold conferences, but they tended to be boring in an amiable way, and his wife and son tried to avoid them. This time he sat at the table with a fresh cup of coffee and smiled up at them, beckoned them to sit down, and said, "What would you guys think about moving?"

Wil said nothing. His mother, who was only slightly thin and had a usually composed face, smiled back nervously and pushed an imaginary hair out of her eyes. "What do you mean?"

"I mean move. You know, like pack up and move."

"Is this another one of those Alaska things?" she asked. Two years before, Wil's father had gotten sick of his job with the state highway department and had come home one day and announced that he had a chance to go to Alaska and work on a road out of Nome and they should start packing. Wil's mother developed a nervous tic in her left eye, which had taken almost a month to disappear. It wasn't as bad as the time a year earlier when he had come home one afternoon and announced he'd come across a plan to raise foxes and retire at forty-six. When he started building the cages in the basement and seemed about to order the first fox, Wil's mother put her foot down. "Because if it is, Jim . . ."

"No, no. This isn't like that. The truth is I've been promoted, and they want me to take over a district in the northern part of the state, up by Pinewood. It's a real opportunity, and I've pretty much got to do it. . . . So how do you guys feel about moving?"

Wil took quick stock of the situation. They now lived in Madison, a fair-size city, with things to do, things to see. All of his friends were here. And he was used to the school, knew which teachers were dorks and which weren't, knew what to expect, knew that he could get through the neighborhood alive . . .

"When?" his mother asked.

"Well . . ." his father hedged.

. . . and knew where the bike shop was to get his Sekai repaired and where to get good hamburgers, knew how to fake volleyball in the phys-ed class to get a good grade, knew which water fountains in school were usually full of gum, which stalls to avoid in the school bathroom . . .

"When?"

"It's kind of different for all of us. I mean, you don't have to go up there when I do. I thought I would sort of go ahead, and then you could kind of follow me when I've found a place. . . ."

. . . knew how to avoid Moose Ackerman, who liked body contact and thought everybody else did, knew which hobby shop had the best models, knew which video store had the best tapes, knew which music outlet had the best albums, knew which roads were best for pacing bikes, knew where Cindy Mattson lived . . .

"When?"

"I'm going up there Saturday, but like I said, you two could come later. Maybe hold back until Monday or even Tuesday."

"Are you crazy?"

. . . knew where Cindy Mattson lived, knew where to buy the best Polish sausage in the world, knew which bookstore had the best games, and finally, had already dissected the fetal pig in biology, which he vowed under pain of death never to do again . . .

"Wait. Wait." His father held up his hand. "I know it's sudden, but there it is, and I have to go. I just found out yesterday that the district administrator up there had personal problems and had to leave. . . ."

"Probably went insane," Wil's mother interrupted. "From the loneliness."

"Oh, come on, it's not that bad. I bet Wil doesn't think it's that bad, do you, Wil?"

Wil was still thinking about the fetal pig and had a fetal-pig-dissecting look on his face, which didn't help to soften the blow of his words. "I've got to be totally honest, Dad—totally honest."

"Well?"

"I think my whole life is going down the toilet."

2

Sometimes old wisdom isn't so good. I complained once about household chores, and my father told me to sing and act happy when I did them even if I didn't feel that way. That's what his grandfather told him to do. So the next time I edged the sidewalk I tried singing "la, la, la" in time with my cutting strokes. As near as I can figure, it didn't help at all, and I came within half a second of being nicknamed "La-La Neuton" as Tim Peterson came down the street from my rear and nearly caught me off guard.

—Wil Neuton

MOVING proved to be easier than they'd expected. After the initial arguing had died down—Wil thought of it as a small, friendly war with no prisoners—his father explained that a house came with the move, a small house located in the center of the district, provided by the state highway department. The old administrator was already moved out. So they rented a truck and loaded up everything in Madison—as near as Wil could figure—and drove one hundred and sixty miles north to unload it.

Of course, there was more to the move than that. It took only four days—and nights—but some major shifting had to be considered. Wil went by Cindy's house three times to tell her he was leaving, but she was already at her lake home with her parents—and while that sad fact probably didn't matter to Cindy, who didn't know Wil well enough to remember his name, it mattered to Wil. His best friend, Judah Timmons, was no help either.

"It's kind of like dying, isn't it?" he said when Wil told him he was moving north. "Kind of like just slowly dying."

"Thanks. For cheering me up."

"You're welcome. Does this mean that I get to try getting Cindy to notice me now? You know, the way you tried to get her to notice you?"

And his second-best friend, or equally best friend, David Collins, was just about as compassionate. "Who are we going to get to ride in front when we pace bikes now? You're the only one big enough to break the wind for all of us. I mean, that destroys the summer. Maybe you could stay here alone and go up next fall. . . ."

But finally, on Sunday evening, they piled into the rental truck, and Wil held a small cage with his tomcat, Bob, in his lap, and they drove north for four and a half hours, winding on small asphalt roads past the farms and into the northern forest, at last turning off the paved roads and taking a gravel road four more winding miles to a yellow house with brown trim that looked a little old but clean in the headlights.

"Home," Wil's father said. He was going to say something else but stopped when he saw the look in his wife's eye.

Wil was sitting on the right side, and he opened the door and got out, put the cat cage down, stretched, then bent over and released Bob, who made a straight, gray-hair-line for the small front porch and scooted beneath it, where he sat emitting a low, throaty growl. He had never spent time in a cage, never ridden in a truck, never had to move, and apparently, Wil judged, didn't think much of any of them.

Leaving the truck lights on, Wil's father went up the porch steps to the front door. "They said they'd leave a key . . . yup, here it is. Isn't that wonderful? They said they'd leave a key and there it is, right where they said they'd leave it."

"Jim . . ." Wil's mother sighed. "Is there some light in there?"

As soon as she said it, the house and the front lawn were flooded with light. The minute his father found the switches every mosquito within miles seemed to hit them. Wil grabbed his mother's arm, ran for the house, and got her inside, both of them slapping and scratching.

"Few mosquitoes," his father said. "But the house has screens."

The house proved to be clean, with decent furniture and a stove that worked. They rummaged around in the truck to find three dishes and some pans and cooked beans and franks and ate them, sitting quietly in their exhaustion. There were beds but no linen, so they spread blankets on them, and Wil took the room nearest the front door. Without taking his clothes off, he sprawled out on his back.

He hurt all over. To the same mental file he had begun for fetal-pig dissections he added being on the downside of a chest freezer that is being carried up from the basement and heavy wooden dressers being carried from upstairs down. At one point, while his father was screaming at him, "Lift! Lift!" he felt as if he were being driven into the ground and was glad he wasn't sharp on the bottom end or they'd never have gotten him out. For a moment he tried to feel sad, tried to summon a mental picture of Cindy or miss his friends, but he was too tired; his eyes closed and he went to sleep listening to the death-whine of mosquitoes against the screen and the low rumble of Bob out underneath the porch.

He did not know what awakened him. One second he was asleep, and the next his eyes were open and he was staring at the ceiling, not realizing where he was or how he got there. The sun was streaming through the windows and cooking his head. He had been sleeping flat on his back, hard and down, without moving and with his mouth open, and now he was awake to a taste that can come only from sleeping with your mouth open after eating half-warm beans and franks, and he couldn't think of where he had packed his toothbrush. He turned his head sideways and saw a face looking at him through the window—a face so ugly it drove him off the bed and down along the wall.

It was an old face, an old man's face, round, with no hair, and ears that stuck out to the side; when the mouth opened in a smile, Wil saw just one tooth, sticking up from the bottom in the middle, and the lips were rimmed with a gummy brown substance that squeezed out at the corners.

The window was open, and the face emitted a sound through the screen which seemed something like "Aucht." Then it disappeared sideways for a moment. There was a great, glopping-spitting racket, and it reappeared, a thin line of brown juice rolling down from the lower lip onto the stubbed chin and Wil thought: *I am going to throw up if I don't quit looking at him.* But he couldn't take his eyes off the face—it was like a live Halloween mask.

"Aucht," the face said again. "Emil Aucht."

Dad, Wil thought, *Mom*, but it didn't come out. He smiled, rose up a little, and pretended to understand. *Probably a maniac*, he thought—*probably a maniac with an ax, and he needs to chop somebody up. That's why the other guy had to leave the house and his job. Ax murderers running around. I'd leave, too.* "Emil?"

Now the face nodded wildly. "Emil Aucht. Nee hep. Stuck." Each word was punctuated by a brown spray that left the screen dripping. Wil had to look away.

But now he knew something. It was a name. Emil Aucht was his name. *Nice name. Nice name for an ax murderer. Probably has a chain saw out there—high-tech ax murderer.* Wil stood and moved carefully along the wall to the door, nodding and smiling all the way, and when he got to the doorway he slid sideways out of the room and almost screamed. "Mom! Dad!"

No answer. In the kitchen there was a note on the table.

Wil: We've run to town for food. You were so tired we thought it best to let you sleep.
Love, Mom.

They found him, Wil imagined, *holding the note from his mother in his hand, the ax buried to the handle in his skull, the walls splattered with* . . . He shook his head.

"Emil Aucht! Stuck! Nee hep!"

Wil turned and saw the man standing now at the open front door, looking at him through the screen. He was wearing bib overalls with no shirt, and there were tufts of hair on the tops of his shoulders. In his right hand he was carrying a shovel, and Wil had a momentary picture of the shovel buried in his skull, with the note in his hand. But he couldn't make the idea of a crazed shovel murderer work, so he walked to the front door.

"Can I help you?"

The question brought wild nodding, and the man gurgled and spat over the side of the porch—a great brown stream that nearly hit Bob, who was coming out to investigate and went back, probably for life, Wil thought—and pointed up the road. Wil leaned against the screen, one eye on the shovel, and looked up the road to where an old pickup was stuck just off the shoulder in the soft mud.

"Oh," Wil said. "You're stuck."

More wild nodding. "Emil Aucht. Nee hep. Stuck." And the man turned and jumped off the porch and started up the road, waving for Wil to follow him. "Youpush. Commhep."

Feeling rather silly, Wil followed. The truck had gone just a few inches too far off the road, and the ditch mud had taken the rear wheel in and down. In the back of the truck was a nondescript small hound with bits of hair gone and dirt stuck here and there, and when Wil came near the tailgate it made a concentrated effort to lick his face without actually leaving the truck, leaning farther and farther out until it was teetering, slobbering like a tongue on the end of a motor.

"Youpush. I driving."

Wil nodded, got in back of the right side, to the rear of the sunken wheel, and settled his shoulder into the tailgate. Now the dog could reach him and stuck a tongue in his ear that felt as if it went halfway through his head at the same time that Emil gunned the engine. There was a mighty spray of mud, most of which splattered the front of his pants and T-shirt and face as the truck lurched, jumped forward, and was gone, leaving Wil facedown on the road, with another entry to add to the list of fetal pigs, chest freezers, and dressers.

He walked slowly back to the house and was just getting to the porch when his father and mother drove up.

"What happened to you?" his mother asked once she got out of the car. "When we left you were asleep. . . ."

"Emil." Wil pointed vaguely down the road. "Stuck. I hep. He driving. Gone. La, la."

With that he went into the house, letting the door slam behind him. Sitting on the edge of his bed, he found a clean spot on his T-shirt—a little patch around to the side where the mud hadn't hit—and used it to swab the dog slobber out of his ear. It was not, he decided, a good start. Perhaps not as bad as it could have been. The dog, for instance, could have had rabies, and Emil could have turned out to be a mad scientist with nuclear capabilities—that might have been worse. But all in all it was not a really good start in the new home.

And this was only the first day.

3.

I wanted to be a jock for a long time. Especially when Cindy decided she liked football players. But I got my hands on my dad's high school yearbook and asked him about what happened to all the football biggies. Almost all of them are either selling cars or running insurance agencies except one, who somehow ran over himself with a boat trailer. So I figured it wasn't worth it, even for Cindy.

—Wil Neuton

W<small>IL</small> cleaned a little in the dirty water that came out of the kitchen tap—the bathroom faucets, mysteriously, did not work.

"Yet," his father responded. "I'll fix them this afternoon."

"Oh, don't worry," his mother said, smiling. She had by now slipped into what Wil called her cheerful, we'll-get-by mode. "We'll get by somehow"—extremely dangerous words because they usually meant that no matter what happened, she would stay happy and cheerful. *Which sounds good*, he thought, but was bad because it threw everybody off—you didn't want somebody running around smiling and saying, "We'll get by," when the house was on fire; you wanted somebody to yell "fire!" Also, the happy mood tended to drive his father completely crazy because his father was most decidedly not a "we'll-get-by" kind of person. The more she smiled and smoothed things, the crazier he became, almost as if he were challenging her.

They had breakfast—eggs and sausage from a cafe in town, eaten out of styrofoam trays. Then his father stood. "Well. Let's unload the truck."

Whereupon they went outside and took everything that had been in Madison, Wisconsin, out of the truck and brought it into the small house, including the chest freezer, which they lugged to the basement with Wil on the bottom as they went down. They stacked and stacked, pushed and pulled, and all the rooms were still piled high with boxes and furniture and dishes. Wil took his ten-speed from the truck and leaned it against a tree in the front yard. But everything else went in the house. Then his father uttered the fateful words that Wil and his mother knew meant impending disaster.

"Now," he said, rubbing his hands together. "Let's take a look at that plumbing. . . ."

Which isn't what he meant. If he meant he were really just going to take a look at it and then call a plumber, that would have been all right. But what he really meant was that he was going to try to fix it. He found his toolbox and, armed with propane torches and pipe wrenches, headed for the basement stairs. "I mean, how complicated can it be? Just a bunch of pipes and water, right? Wil, you come help me."

La, Wil thought—*la, la*—heading for the basement

with him. Three times in his life he had witnessed his father versus plumbing. It was never pretty, although he had learned some interesting new words that his father apparently had been saving for plumbing ever since he'd been in the army. But on the third attempt, when a weak relief valve on the water heater had let go just at the wrong instant and shot a jet of hot water up his pants leg, the neighbors had actually called because they thought somebody was abusing a pet animal of some kind.

"Dad, I noticed one of the spokes was bent on my bike. Maybe I should get on that right away. . . ."

But his father was lost to the plumbing, following the pipes through the exposed basement ceiling. "Let's see, they go over here, then carry the water up here, then around here, then carry the water up here, then around here, over that way—yes. I see the problem. Ri-i-ight here." He put a wrench on a joint, gave a small tug, and, when nothing happened, gave a larger jerk. There was a thunderous explosion of water as the joint let go, a powerful stream hit his father in the face and drove him back and down against the wall—already sputtering some of the more famous Plumbing Curses—and Wil went up the basement stairs.

"Mom, Mom. You'd better call a plumber. Pretty fast."

Water was spraying all over the room now as the pipe hung down from the ceiling and waved back and forth, and his father was on his hands and knees, wielding the pipe wrench like a knight with a sword looking for a wet dragon to kill. Near the pump, in the corner, Wil saw a large valve that looked like it might do something, and he tightened it down. It proved to be the main shutoff and stopped the water.

"Yeah," his father said, crouching. "Kill it. That's the way. Kill it. Don't let it get up now, kill it."

"It's all right, Dad. It's all right. I turned it off."

"Oh, oh . . ." His father's eyes cleared. The dragons went away. He stood, dripping into the small lake on the floor. "Oh, yes—plumbing, right?"

"Right."

"Did your mother call a plumber?"

"I think so. I yelled at her to call one."

"Good, that's good. I don't have time for this anyway. We have to get moved in. . . ."

"Right."

Just then his mother came to the top of the steps and called down. "There aren't any plumbers available in either Maypine or Pinewood. So I called the store, and they said there is a kind of general handyman they use and they said they'd send him around."

I know this part, Wil thought, closing his eyes. She almost doesn't need to say it. I know what's coming. . . .

"It's a man named Emil something. The woman coughed when she said his last name. Oh, Emil—say, Wil, isn't that the name of the man you helped out of the ditch while we were gone?"

Wil looked up at his mother and down at his father and wondered if there was a way to warn them, tell them. He decided there was nothing he could say that would prepare them for Emil. They wouldn't believe him anyway—you pretty much had to see Emil to believe him. "Yes. Well. I have that ten-speed bike problem to get on. Then I guess I'll take a test ride. Catch you guys later, all right?"

He went upstairs and out into the yard. His ten-speed did have a bent spoke, but it wasn't bad, and he straightened it with his fingers rather than going through the hassle of taking the tire off and replacing it. Then he kicked his toe clips up, worked his feet into the pedals, and started pedaling.

He wasn't sure where to go, and the gravel road was hard to ride on with his one-inch tires. But he found that if he stayed in the packed tire lane where the cars ran it wasn't too bad, and soon he was up to cadence, pumping through the noon sun down a country road bordered by poplar trees.

It always cleared his mind to ride, no matter what was bothering him, and he held cadence until his forehead was covered with sweat and his legs and knees had the tingling ache that comes with good exercise and he was pulling air in great lungfuls. When he got to that stage, he looked up; he was going past a small lake, and in the middle of the lake there was an island.

Later he was not sure why he had stopped. He had seen many lakes, and many islands, and this was not a particular pretty lake or island. As a matter of fact, the south end of the lake, where the road passed, was low and swampy—which was why brush didn't obscure his view of the island—and not particular pretty at all.

He sat up, letting the bicycle glide, and looked over the lake. The road curved up and around and away, and just before the lake was out of sight he stopped and turned and wheeled the bike back. He had passed what appeared to be a small path or trail; when he got back to it he turned off and leaned the bike against a tree and walked down through some poplars to the edge of the lake. Here there was a broken old dock and, pulled up on shore, an old wooden boat and two splintery hardwood oars. The boat was filled with rainwater and clearly hadn't been used in years. But it was made of cedar strips and had not rotted, and it came into Wil's mind that he should take the boat and go out to the island.

That's the way it came—just a slight thought, a gentle little thought to nudge him. But it stuck, and he pulled and rocked at the boat until the water was sloshing back and forth, and with a great heave he got the boat up on its side and emptied it. There was moss, algae grown into corners, but it was still sound and he pushed it onto the water near the rotted dock until the boat was floating. It would need a rope, which he didn't have, but he pulled it back up until it was held by the mud. Then he looked at the oars.

They were cracked, but they had been made of oak and though warped were still usable. They had alloy pins that hadn't rusted; the fittings on the boat were of the same alloy, and he slipped the pins in the locks and laid the oars along the sides of the boat in readiness. Then he went back up to his bicycle and moved it farther off into the brush, covered it with some branches, and returned to the boat.

It took him only a minute to jump in, push off with an oar, and get settled on the old dry seat in the middle. As heavy as it was, water-soaked for years, the boat still moved easily to the oars, and in ten more minutes he was bumping against the small rocks at the south edge of the island.

He hopped out, standing in the water in his tennis shoes, and skinned the boat up onto the rocks. Then he turned it on its side and stuck the oars up inside and turned and looked around.

"See," he said aloud. "See what I have found—an island all for myself." He felt only a little strange talking to himself, and he smiled and walked along the shore wondering why he had taken the boat out to the island in the first place; what pull had brought him? He had seen other islands, yet there was something about this one. It . . . fit him, somehow. Seemed to fit him.

He went to the right and soon was up on the north end of the right side of the U, where he turned left, started around the corner, and came to the large, square table rock that jutted out into the bay. Two mallards lifted off the bay—a male, all green-headed with white wing flecks, and a dappled gray-brown female—and Wil jumped when they took off. There were birds singing, and some insect sound, but the sun was keeping the mosquitoes down and the quiet was very peaceful.

He walked onto the rock and sat on the outer edge, letting his feet dangle over the side. His heels almost touched the water, and when he rocked his toes forward they just broke the surface; some small sunfish came to investigate the disturbance, which might be a meal. They hovered in the shade of the rock, darted in and out with each ripple, flashed their sides in the sun, golden blinks that came up through the water into Wil's eyes and into his mind.

He sat for some time, watching the fish, looking across the bay, listening to the birds, and the place felt, in a way, like home. It felt like he was supposed to be there, and when he stood and brushed the rock dust off his pants and walked back to the boat, some of the day was gone.

But the newness filled him, and he did not think of Madison or feel lonely as he rowed back to the main shore, left the boat upside down in the brush, found his bike, and got out on the road. He did not think of Madison or his friends there; he thought only of the island, the sunfish coming to his toes, the mallards jumping into the sky the way they did, the sun, the birds.

And he knew he would come back. He knew it with a kind of basic, fundamental knowledge; he would breathe in and out—and he would come back to the island.

4

Great discoveries don't always mean that much. I was there the day Jimmy Baskin found that the dents in his skull were different from the dents in everybody else's skull; he figured he'd discovered a whole new way of identifying people. Like fingerprints, they could do skullprints. He was amazed by it and ran around the school feeling everybody's skull, looking for different dents, until he grabbed Moose Ackerman's head by mistake. Moose body-contacted him almost completely through a gym locker and put two new dents in Jimmy's skull, and there went his great discovery. Jimmy figures if it was that easy to change the skull-dent pattern his theory wouldn't hold up.

—Wil Neuton

WIL arrived home just at evening, as the bugs started to come out. He put his bike against the tree in the yard and went up the steps and into the house.

His father was standing there, holding a floor lamp, trying to decide where to put it in the almost impossibly crowded small living room. "Hi. Where've you been?"

"Just out for a run on the bike. Went farther than I

thought I would." Suddenly, for no real reason, he did not want to speak of the island. It wasn't a secret, just a private place, a thing he did not understand yet and he did not want to talk about it. "Is everything all right here?"

"Sort of . . ."

"What's the matter?"

"Nothing. The guy came and fixed the plumbing. Short guy with a bald head and chewing snoose all the time, hair out his shoulders . . ."

"And a dog that goobers in your ear. That's Emil Aucht."

"Yeah. That's the one. I got too close to his truck and the dog got me. He came and fixed the plumbing."

"So what's the matter?"

"It's your mother—she's in the kitchen."

Wil went across the room and into the kitchen, where his mother was leaning over the sink, scrubbing with a sponge, her eyes closed while the hot water poured. She looked up when Wil walked in. "You could have told me . . ."

"Told you what?"

"Told me we'd have to boil the whole house after he left." Her face was gray. "I mean he walked over and spit in the sink. Just walked over and let go with this big . . ." She couldn't finish. "I'll never get the sink clean, never. And the basement looks like the inside of a spittoon. I don't dare go down there."

Wil nodded. "Sounds like Emil, all right. You're lucky he spit in the sink. Did you meet his dog? Nice dog . . ."

"You could have told us," she said. "That's the least you could have done."

Wil shrugged. "You wouldn't have believed me. Nobody would believe me. *I* didn't believe me. What's for supper?"

"Wil! How can you think of food?'

"It's easy. I'm hungry. I'll just get a can of stew or something and eat it cold, all right?" He opened some cupboards and found pans and pots and finally opened the pantry and found the canned goods. There was no stew. He took a can of beans, found the opener, and was putting it back when he saw that Bob was under the sink. Still growling, but in the house.

"Bob! It's good to see you. . . ."

The cat ignored him, and his mother had gone back to cleaning the sink and would probably be cleaning it this time tomorrow, so Wil took the beans and a spoon back out to the front steps and sat, eating, slapping a mosquito now and then as they grew bolder.

He would need a small rope for the boat, and a notebook. He wasn't sure why he'd need the notebook but felt that the island demanded it. And he could use his small waist pack to carry food out there. Tomorrow he would go back and sit on the rock again. It was a place, he decided—a place he liked. A place he liked to be.

"Hi."

Wil looked up directly into the sun, which was setting and hit him straight from the road, and he couldn't see anything. Somebody had come off the road. He could make out a form, but he couldn't see who it was. He moved his head sideways, squinted, and finally had to put the beans down and stand and let the flash of the sun fade from his retinas.

"I was biking by and saw you sitting there. You must be the new people. I'm Susan."

Wil found himself looking down at a girl with short,

reddish-brown hair and wide brown eyes that had flecks of green in them somehow. She was thin, about a head shorter than Wil, and was wearing a T-shirt and jeans. Across the front of the T-shirt there was a small band of old people, playing drums and a clarinet and an accordion, and beneath that, in large block letters, it said: WISCONSIN—HOME OF PUNK POLKA.

"I'm Wil," he said, suddenly shy. "Wil Neuton. Yeah, we're the new people."

"Your dad must work for the highway department." Susan had been holding a ten-speed, and she let it slide to the grass, where it rested on the bars and one pedal. "It's the highway department's house."

Wil nodded. "Yeah." *I'm being dumb here*, he thought. *Just yeah, yeah—kind of sounds like la, la. I don't want to be dumb here.* "We're just moving in. . . ." *Smart*, he thought, *really smart.*

"We live down the road," she said, pointing with her chin. "I saw you go by on your bike a while ago. You were really moving."

"Just setting cadence. You know, pumping up."

"Really moving," she repeated. "We'll have to bike together."

"Yeah." *Oh God, I might as well commit suicide. The next time Emil comes by I'll stick my head in the back of his truck and let the dog lick me to death.* "I mean, yes—I'd like that."

She studied him, her head cocked to one side. "You know, you're really being hard to talk to. Kind of like pulling teeth. Are you always this way?"

"No. Yes. I mean no . . ."

"Just shy around girls?"

Wil didn't say anything. *I'm dead either way*, he thought.

If I admit it, I'm history; if I come right out and lie, I might as well say "yeah" again.

"That's what I thought. Shy around girls. I'll bet you're fifteen, aren't you?"

He nodded, smiling a little now. "Yup." Only a little better than "yeah"—but better.

"So am I. But it takes boys different. My brother is seventeen, but I remember when he was fifteen and a girl came over and he just about swallowed his tongue. Then his voice broke up and he got pimples and a car, and it was all over. He isn't shy anymore. I mean you should see him. He sees a girl and he's gone, just gone." She laughed. "We run a dairy farm, and he has to help Dad milk before and after school, and if there's a girl around he might just put the milking machine on the wrong end of the cow."

"Sounds wild." Wil ran a hand through his hair. "Your brother, I mean . . ."

"There. You can open up and talk. That's good. I have to go now, but maybe tomorrow or the next day we could take a bike ride, and you could show me how to do that cadence thing—is that all right?"

And she was gone—she picked up the bike and was gone before Wil could say anything more, do anything more. He watched her ride off down the road, throwing a wave back at him over her shoulder, and he waved but she couldn't see it.

"Nice girl," his mother said, coming out on the porch. "What's her name?"

"Susan. She didn't say her last name."

His mother sat down on the top step and wiped her forehead. "This move hasn't been really easy on anybody, but it hit you kind of hard, didn't it?"

Wil didn't say anything for a time, then he shook his head. "No. It was something Dad had to do, and I miss my friends, but, you know, it's not so bad. We didn't have to do Alaska, and some kids have to move all the time. I knew a kid named Raymond who had a father in the army, and the longest he was in a school was one year—sometimes he'd do two and three schools a year. I've been lucky."

"He's a good man, your father."

"Yes. I know."

"Sometimes he does things fast, but he's a good man."

This time Wil said nothing. There was nothing to say.

"This is kind of a nice place, isn't it?" She stood and put her hand on the porch screen door. "Clean and nice. The air, I mean. And the sound of the birds. Kind of nice."

Then she went back in and left Wil sitting, still looking down the road where Susan had gone, thinking of nothing, everything, listening to the evening sounds start, the mosquitoes coming, the night birds tuning up, his father swearing at the plumbing.

Swearing at the plumbing? He stood and went up the steps. It was supposed to be fixed. Something else must have broken or he wouldn't be coming loose again.

I'll just drop down there and give him a hand, Wil thought. *La, la.*

5

Lying doesn't seem to be worth the effort. I once had a phys-ed teacher who insisted that I make up an hour of weight lifting I had missed by working it off five minutes each day after school. Well, I'm not a weight-lifting kind of person. As a matter of fact, I'm more of a weight-putting-down kind of person. I hate lifting weights. And it was silly the way he wanted the time made up. I would have my friends wait in the hall and run in and lift like crazy for five minutes, then again the next night, and the next. . . . Finally I skipped the last four or five or six sessions and told the teacher I had done them, and that would have been all right except that it ate at me, and ate at me, and ate at me. I must have come from a gene pool that had a lot of guilt chromosomes. So I took to stopping on my own when nobody was around and lifting weights. To kind of make up for lying. And once I started, I kept at it, and I forgot how many five-minute sessions I had missed and I know I went way over. All told and added up, I must have lifted over twelve tons for that one small lie. I might as well have told the truth and just gotten the job done. I know my back would have liked it better, and what am I going to do with overdeveloped biceps?

—Wil Neuton

WIL loved riding early in the morning. Back in Madison he sometimes would get up just before dawn and fill his water bottle and take off out into the country on a forced hundred-kilometer ride—driving through the morning light, pumping in the mist, and listening to the birds sing, the end of night songs and the start of day songs.

This morning he awakened before dawn, or when the first light was beginning to gray up his bedroom window. Robins were singing, and sparrows and some doves were opening the day when Wil went into the kitchen. His parents were still asleep, and he tiptoed on his tennis shoes to keep from waking them. It was not unusual for him to go out early, and he scribbled a note on a piece of paper sack saying that he was biking and would be gone all day. He found some cans of food— one pineapple chunks, one can of stew—and an opener on the blade of a pocket knife, which he dropped into his pocket. He put a bowl of food down for Bob, who had now come out from under the sink but was still decidedly mad, and let the front screen close silently behind him.

His bike was leaning against the wall where he'd left it the night before. He pushed it out onto the road. Then he tied on the waist pack, threw a leg over the seat, toed the pedal clips up, and started down the road— into the sun, the new sun. He let the front wheel find the hard parts of the road and pedaled easily for a mile or so, sitting almost upright, the wind working through his hair.

After his legs loosened, he curved over and picked

up the cadence and rode fast for another half mile. Then a large truck, a milk truck with a shiny stainless steel tank on the back, came up behind him, and he pulled over and let it go by—on the way to Susan's place to pick up milk, he figured.

The island was very strong in his mind now, calling him, pulling him. As soon as the milk truck passed, he picked up speed again and held it until he came around the shallow curve and saw the end of the lake, then the island.

Still in the mist, it sat in the mirrored water as if floating on the lake, floating in a sky land of water and fluffy clouds. Wil pulled the bike onto the trail and hid it in the brush. It took him a minute to tip the boat over and slide it into the water. Then he got the oars ready, put the pack down in the bow, turned the boat around, and began rowing. Halfway to the island he stopped, let the oars hang, and sat silently.

Ripples made by the boat widened across the glass of the surface and disappeared, leaving it smooth, gentle, still. *I am a painting*, he thought. *I can sit still this way and the boat is part of the water and I am part of the boat and the sky and I am a painting.* He closed his eyes for a moment and held his breath until no part of him moved, until the boat was completely still. Then he opened his eyes and saw the lake, and in back of the boat, in the new morning sun, a bass flicked the surface and left a perfect circle of a ripple that moved out and out. And he breathed it, breathed the word "perfect."

And it hit him then that there had been no time in his life when he could think that, when he could say that, could say there had been a perfect moment. It faded slowly, birds filled it with sound, more fish jumped;

and when it was done, when the still perfection was finished, he rowed the rest of the way to the island. This time, instead of pulling up at the southern, outside curve, he pulled the boat around the outside edge and into the small bay.

A loon with two nearly grown chicks dived in the middle of it. But they didn't stay down long, coming up before they had gone more than forty feet, watching the boat as he pulled onto the sand next to the table rock. Wil slid the boat well up out of the water and turned it over, leaning it against the rock to make a leaning shelter.

The sun was well up now, heating the bay and rock, and he sat on the end of the flat surface and took off his shirt, letting the heat soak into his back and shoulders. For a time his mind was blank, free. He watched the loons, sitting still, watching him. The mother studied him openly, wary, diving now and again and surfacing slightly to the side to cock her head. Wil sat quietly, moving only his eyelids, and she became accustomed to him. The chicks sensed her relaxation and moved in closer to the rock.

It was all like this once, Wil thought, watching the loon and her chicks. *All of everything was this way at one time. A person could sit next to a loon, and the loon would not know fear and would come close. That is part of why I am here*, he thought, *because it was all like this once, and it should be all like this again.* A mosquito landed on his hand, and he sat perfectly still until the mosquito found the right place and started to insert its proboscis; then Wil moved his hand and the mosquito flew.

But the hand movement was enough to get the attention of the mother loon, and she froze, then dove, and the chicks followed. And Wil thought: *For that instant I was not perfect. No, that's wrong—I will never be perfect. For that instant I was not correct, not trying to achieve . . . achieve what? Perfection? No.* It wasn't that, it wasn't seeking perfection that brought him to the island. It was more a finding of peace, and he didn't know he needed peace. A finding of harmony—that was it, harmony.

There was more here that he did not understand, but he wanted to know. He wanted to know—he wanted to know the loons. Right now he wanted to know the loons and to know all that he could find out about the loons; he wanted to sit and watch them and learn what they were and know them. And if perfection came from that, if harmony came from that, if knowledge came from that, from his being on the island, that was fine. But he wanted to know the loons. This day, his first day on the island, his first full, real day, he would try to learn the loons, learn what made them part of the island as he wanted to be part of the island.

Another mosquito landed on his hand, and this time he did not move. He let the mosquito drink and pull his blood until its abdomen was swollen and red with blood. And the mosquito flew away, and still he did not move. Wil watched the loons all of that morning, watched them play and swim and feed, watched them rest and play and feed again, watched their dance with the bay, with the water, with the sun and sky and wind. The sun burned him; he did not eat or drink—did not feel the need—and when, finally, in the afternoon he unbent stiffly and stood, stretching the ache away, he had no idea how long he had been there.

He was, instantly it seemed, empty with hunger, and

he found the pack under the boat where he'd left it. He opened a can of stew and took a spoon from the pack and ate quietly. When he was done, he rinsed the can out and put it back in his pack. Then he took off his shorts and walked into the water until it was waist deep. With a gentle shove he slid off on his stomach and swam in a slow, floating crawl. The loons moved away when he went into the water, and he didn't want to bother them, so he just swam the heat off his back and circled around to the rock, where he pulled himself out of the water and dried with his T-shirt. He looked once more around the bay, then rolled the boat over and put it in the water and rowed evenly, silently back to shore and his bike.

It had been a long, and strangely short, day. He would have to think long about it and try to decide what had happened.

6.

*Adults can be so strange. It's almost as if they have their own
natural laws that have nothing to do with the natural laws the
rest of us use. I had an uncle once who told me I was a fool for
playing D&D one whole weekend at Brennan Weise's house.
Which might have been the truth because we almost got into a
fight that night when Brennan's elf got snarked by the dragon
and he didn't have any spells to use. But later the same uncle
played poker with my dad and some other guys all of one night
and the next day and part of the next night, all for pennies;
and when he was done, he had lost sixty cents and said he had
fun even though his eyes looked like two glowing cigar ends. So
who was foolish? At least I didn't lose sixty cents, and my elf
didn't get snarked.*

—Wil Neuton

"**H**I." The voice almost knocked him off his
bicycle. He had been pumping hard, head down, trying
to get home before dark, and as he passed the end of
a driveway the voice came from behind a mailbox and
caught him completely off guard. "Hi."

He raised his head and pulled the brakes and turned

to find Susan standing in the half-light. It was cooling, and she had on a windbreaker. Her bike was leaning against the mailbox post.

"Oh," he said. "It's you. Hi." He breathed deeply, catching his wind. "I didn't see you until I was almost past. Sorry. How you doing?"

"You can talk nice, see?" She smiled. "It's just a matter of relaxing. Then you aren't so shy."

Which of course made him shy again, but he shrugged it off. He wasn't as he'd been before—something to do with the day on the island. Something to do with his mind. The long, peaceful day. "Are you going for a ride?" he asked, pointing at her bike. "An evening ride?"

She hesitated, thinking. "Well. I saw you go by this morning and thought I'd follow you. But by the time I told my folks and got my bike, you were out of sight. But I followed your tracks in the dust of the road and saw where you turned off by Sucker Lake. Then I found your bike and saw that the minnow boat was gone."

"Minnow boat?" Wil held up his hand. "What's a minnow boat?"

She shook her hair and smiled at his ignorance. "That's the boat you took. All these lakes used to have minnow traps where men would get bait to sell to tourists. Every lake had an old boat and oars to go out to the minnow traps. The traps are gone, but the old boats weren't worth taking away, so they left them. That's the boat you took out to the island."

Wil was off his bike now, standing with the seat against his hip. "You saw me go to the island?"

She nodded. "Well, not really. I saw the boat gone and found your bike, and when I went up along the shore I saw you sitting on that flat rock, but it was too

37

far away to see what you were doing. What were you doing?"

Again Wil felt embarrassed that she had seen him, but again it went quickly. "I'm not sure."

"You were there long enough for not knowing what you were doing. I went off for a ride and came back, and you were still there. And I waited and waited, but you were still there, so I came back here and waited."

For a time neither of them said anything, looking down. It was a silence that grew into something neither of them had planned. *I wonder why she watched and waited that long*, Wil thought. *What a strange thing to do. Why would she wait that long for me?* "You should have called," he said. "I would have come back to the shore."

She shrugged. "You were busy—I could see that. Why don't I ride back to your house with you? You could show me that cadence thing."

Wil nodded, glad that she wanted to be with him, and waited until she got her bike on the road. Then they rode off side by side. He showed her how to set a cadence and keep at the rhythm until she had steady speed and was making the most efficient use of her muscles and the gear ratio on her bike. In no time they were at his driveway. He slowed and turned in and stopped.

"Well. I'm home."

She nodded and stopped next to him. "Yes. You are. So . . . I'll see you." She turned to go, and he thought how rude it was to make her ride home alone just as he realized that he did not want her to go yet. "Wait," he pulled his bike back out on the road. "I'll go home with you."

She laughed. "We'll just keep going back and forth all night. Don't worry, I'll be all right." She was gone before he could protest again, and he decided it would be wrong to push it, so he waved and watched until she was out of sight in the evening light. Then he leaned his bike against the house and went in. His mother and father were sitting in the kitchen table with cups of coffee. They looked up when he came in.

"Sit down, Wil," his father said. "We've got to have a talk."

Oh good, Wil thought, *one of those. Last time he said it that way we tried getting rich growing cauliflowers in our back yard. No, that was the time before. Last time it was the foxes—or was it the chinchillas? Those were the furry little buggers who had so many thousand hairs per square inch that air couldn't get in or something, hairs that either never split or split all the time. No, no, that was two times ago, or three times. Last time he had that look we almost moved to Alaska. Wrong again. Last time he had that look we moved here. Four days ago. Really—just four days ago. Only four days. And now there's the island and now there's Susan, and now I am not the same any longer.*

Wil sat down. "What happened? Emil come again to fix the plumbing?"

For a moment his mother and father were silent. His father's face wore a confident look, while his mother's expression had altered slightly, was more questioning or slightly puzzled, as if she weren't sure what was happening. Still they said nothing, and Wil was about to ask about dinner when his father leaned forward across the table and said one word.

"Berries."

Wil thought a moment, then shrugged. "It doesn't scan. I was going to say 'straw' or 'razz,' but it doesn't work. What does it mean?"

"It means we are living in the blueberry and raspberry capital of the world, is what it means. It means I think we have found a way to become independent . . . well, in the long haul. I have to keep working for a time, of course. But we can pick up a small amount of land pretty cheap and plant berries, and people will come from miles around to pick them. It's a lead-pipe cinch, is what it is. . . ."

"Dad, we've only been here four days. . . ."

"That has nothing to do with it. I worked today and asked around, and there aren't any berry farms within a hundred miles of here. People will come all the way up from Madison to pick them, down from Superior. Pinewood Berries will be famous for size and quality."

"Pinewood Berries?"

"He already has a name," Wil's mother put in. "He had the name when he came home from work today. Emil was here to fix the plumbing again, as you guessed, and I was just getting ready to hose out the kitchen when he came in with the name for the berry farm. Or ranch. Is it 'ranch'?"

"Farm, dear. Farm. Out west it would be a berry ranch or berry spread, but up here in the north it's a berry farm. Neuton's Pinewood Berry Farm. Catchy name, isn't it?"

Wil nodded. "Catchy."

His mother nodded. "Catchy."

"Look, I know you guys are just being nice to me. And I know I've come up with some harebrained ideas in the past. But this time it's different, honest. This looks good. Not for a year or two, but then it should kick in. People will pick their own berries and pay us, and we can be self-sufficient. Kind of a back-to-the-land thing."

"Well . . ." His mother paused. "I think it could be a good thing. But let's go slow, shouldn't we? I mean let's not jump into it." She stood. "And now I should get supper. I have some meat loaf made and mushroom gravy. . . ."

"I thought I smelled something good," Wil said, standing and going to wash his hands. Bob was under the bathroom sink now and snarled lightly when he came into the bathroom—almost happy-sounding. Wil reached down to pet him, and Bob took a halfhearted swipe at him, but he was obviously mellowing and missed by a mile.

At the table, while Wil and his mother ate, there was much talk of berries, straw, razz, and blue. And when they had eaten and gone into the living room and turned on the television—they had found they got only one channel, the kind that shows old movies and polka parties—and the berry talk died down, Wil coughed to get their attention.

"I found something today," he said. "Or yesterday, but today I went back to it and found something."

"What are you talking about?" His mother looked from the screen, where an ancient country-and-western star was selling an album of his greatest gospel hits to the accompaniment of an organ so drippy it almost drew flies. "What kind of a thing did you find?"

"Well, it's an island. I found an island in a lake not too far from here. It's a small lake and a small island shaped kind of like a horseshoe or something, and I found an old boat and went out to it and sat on this rock, this big square rock, and a thing happened. . . ."

But the ad was over by this time, and his parents had gone back to watching the show—a cop show with a lot of action—and Wil let it slide off. It wasn't so important right now that they know what he had found on the island. He didn't know himself what he had found. But he had told them, that was the most important thing.

He had told them of the island.

7

I used to worry a lot about love. What caused it, why I didn't have it—or rather why I seemed to have it, like with Cindy, only she didn't feel love for me, or wouldn't know if I got run over by a truck in front of her house, which is the same as saying she didn't feel love for me, in a way. Of course I didn't love her, either, but I thought I did then, and I didn't know about love and it would leave me pretty puzzled. So I used to have this aunt named Pam. Well, I still have her but she's down in En-senada or somewhere living with an artist, and nobody talks about her much. I wrote her a letter one day when it was really bad and I asked her about love, how you knew about it, what it was, all of it. For a long time I didn't get anything back at all, and I thought maybe she had forgotten or just not bothered. Then I got a note from her, a postcard, which was kind of em-barrassing because it came to the house in Madison, and Mom and Dad saw it. On the card she told me that if I was talking about sex things there wasn't enough room on the card, and she didn't know what to tell me anyway, but if I meant real love, what she called gut-love, I would know when it came. I would just know. She said love was a lot like having money or reli-gion, people who really had it didn't talk about it. It was just there. Which didn't help me at all, really, but is nice to know.

—Wil Neuton

AGAIN he got up early, just after four. The robins were going crazy, and the sun poured, almost as golden liquid, into the room and across his bed. He rolled out and put his feet on the floor and nearly started to sing himself. He stood and pulled on shorts and tennis shoes and a T-shirt and headed for the kitchen.

It took him a moment to find a can of beans and another of soup, then another minute to leave a note. This time he told them where he was going.

Mom, Dad—I've gone to the island for the day.
See you this evening.

He found a notebook on the table near the television stand, the spiral kind with fifty or so pages. He put that and a pencil in his pack with the beans and soup, then rinsed the spoon he'd had the day before and put it back in the pack. Bob rubbed his leg, openly affectionate and hungry, and Wil sprinkled some dry cat food in a bowl in the corner by the cabinets and poured some water in another bowl. Then he took his pack and slipped quietly outside, letting the screen door close gently.

It was going to be a hot day. Barely past dawn, there was a mugginess in the air that made it thick, and after five minutes of pedaling he was soaked with sweat. As he passed Susan's driveway he slowed, half hoping to see her, but there was nobody, and he picked up speed again. Part of him wanted to see her, and part of him wanted to be alone, but the parts were like two separate people and did not seem in conflict. He just accepted his feelings as they were and let them flow on. That's how he thought of it—let them flow on.

Beyond Susan's there was a slight curve to the right in the road, around a small swamp, and as he came past the curve he startled a deer up ahead. It was a buck, his antlers just out of velvet, and he froze for half a second while the bike went by, then exploded in a bound that took him off the road and into the willows, so that by the time Wil stopped and turned, just hit the brakes and wheeled around, there was no indication the buck had ever been there. Even the branches of the willows where he had gone in were still, and there was not a sound—nothing.

It could have never happened. The thought stuck in Wil's head. The beauty of the deer, the suddenness of the encounter, the leap, the arc of reddish summer fur as the deer vanished in the bright green of the willow leaves, the *sussh* of his breath as he snorted to clear the road, the explosive energy of his back legs kicking him up and through the air and down into the willows—it could have never happened, except for the lingering picture in Wil's mind, the burned beauty of the picture in his brain.

And if there was no indication that it had happened, it was possible that in truth it hadn't. That he dreamed it or imagined it or just wanted it to happen.

But it had happened, and he shook his head and got the bike moving again and in twenty minutes was at Sucker Lake.

The water was like a smooth extension of the sky. When he turned the boat over, one of the oars fell against the side with a thump that echoed and reechoed across the lake; the sound frightened a great blue heron that had been hunting in the reeds nearby, and it lifted off with a gentle flapping of huge wings and slow grace. The gray-blue giant made one circle out across the lake, or half a circle, then flew out of sight over the island. Just before he was gone from view he set his wings in the landing glide, and Wil guessed that he was going to land in the bay on the other side. If he rowed carefully and quietly, he might see the bird again.

Wil pushed the boat in and loaded the pack and began rowing. The problem with rowing was that he had to sit backward, facing away from the direction he wanted to go. Halfway across he decided to switch, which he did, so that he sat and rowed by pushing, looking over the bow. It was much slower, but after a bit he could keep the motion smooth and quiet, and he rowed the rest of the way to the island, watching ahead as he went. The boat cut the water like a silent knife.

When he reached the southern edge of the island, he stepped into the water carefully, pulled the boat up onto the rocky shore as quietly as possible, and with his pack in his hand tiptoed cautiously through the poplars and willows until he could see into the bay.

What he saw was from another time. The loon was there with her two chicks, and they were playing as they had before. Wil stopped and froze and watched, and in a few moments he made out the shape of the blue heron in the reeds to the side, up by the square rock. The heron was absolutely still, standing on long legs, its head solid as it watched the water, hunting, waiting, studying; then, with a movement as quick as a striking snake, the head darted down and he had a frog in his long beak; a flip, the frog turned from sideways to head down into the heron's throat, and he was gone; and the heron was still again, watching, waiting.

I know nothing of that, Wil thought. *I didn't know that herons ate frogs or that they hunted that way; I didn't know or think of what it is like to live as a frog, or a heron, to live and die in a small bay, or how a heron thinks or a loon thinks or if a frog thinks at all. I do not know anything, really, of what I have just seen.*

Nothing.

There came over him then an intense empty feeling, a feeling that he would come to think of later many times as a great thirst or hunger, a great roaring thirst to know more of things, to know more of everything. It started then, or had started with the loons, except that he hadn't understood it or recognized it. But it grew out of him so rapidly that he decided then, while he watched the heron with the loons swimming out in the bay, he decided then to know as much as he could, decided to fill all of the parts of his mind with knowledge.

He would start with the heron.

He kneeled carefully in the grass and willows and took the notebook and pencil out of his pack. At the top of the first page he wrote "HERON" all in capital letters, and beneath that he wrote, "The heron is a large blue bird," and he stopped. He studied the heron, shook his head. In spite of its name, it wasn't a blue bird at all. It was more a slatey gray, almost a metallic gray, with a sheen that caught the sun's light when the bird turned its head to track a passing frog or minnow.

Wil folded the notebook, and on his hands and knees he crept closer to the edge of the water, until he had cut in half the distance to the heron. Then he lay on his stomach and opened the notebook once again, and after studying the bird for several minutes he wrote, "The great blue heron isn't blue. It is a grayish bird, slate gray, with small feathers on the neck that shine like metal in the sun and larger feathers on its wings and body that sometimes seem flat and made of steel. It has long legs, longer than its body, and an equally long neck that coils and moves like a snake so it can aim its beak—which is almost like a spear—all around without moving its body."

And all morning he worked, studying, writing. The heron hunted the whole south edge of the bay and had no idea that Wil was with him, sometimes crawling, sometimes slithering on his stomach. Wil saw many other things, sometimes one thing would lead to two others, and he made side notes about them and would come back to them; but the whole morning he worked on the heron, wrote about the heron, did sketches of the heron, studied the heron. And when the sun was high overhead, he moved backward into the willows and opened a can of pears and tried to be quiet, but the clunking of the can opener carried across the water and into the reeds where the heron hunted. It swiveled its sharp head to locate the sound, then flew with a coarse squawk, making a circle over the bay before it flapped out of sight, looking prehistoric.

Wil watched it leave, disappointed that his clumsiness had frightened it away. He would have to fit in better, learn to not make those noises. When he finished the pears, he drank the juice and put the empty can back in his pack and went out to sit on the square rock. The loons were there and moved away in the small bay, but they knew him a little now and were not frightened so much as just careful.

Wil leaned back on the rock and lay on his back in the sun and let his mind roll. The heron had been something—the way the head had darted to grab the frog, and again and again later to take two small fish, minnows really. Clean movements, graceful, almost dancing movements, very fast but with almost perfect grace.

He stood, curving his arms, back, and legs, trying to become the line of the heron, trying to make the grace and elegance with his body, but he could not make the curves right. The heron was all curves, all curves leading to the sharpness of the beak, all curves focused into the sharp hunting beak, and Wil could not make the curve quite right. He warped his arms and bent his back and moved in a circle; and there was one point, one tiny point, where he looked down at his reflection in the water and could see it, could see the line of the heron, the curve of the heron that led down to his beak, to the hunting beak. And then it was gone, gone as the heron was gone, a second of rightness and it was gone.

But he did not feel bad about it now, as he had earlier. For that moment he had captured the line of the heron with his body, with his mind. He sat back with his notebook and tried to make a sketch of what he had done with his body, of what he had seen in the reflection of the water, but he was not an artist and had to spend many pages drawing lines just to find the right curve, the right curves that he had seen in the water. When he had the curves he tried to fill them in, but that took many more pages; and when the drawings were not quite right, he tried to write more about the heron, and that took still more pages. And he realized he could sit and write and draw and dance the heron, just the heron, for all the pages of all the rest of his life and not understand it.

He could spend all of what he was just on the heron, on every small part of the heron, on the curve of the heron, the flat metallic feathers of the heron, the dance of the heron, the colors of the heron, and still not know the heron. *As for that,* he thought, *as for that I could spend all the rest of my life on just the frog the heron ate, just the small frog the rest of my time. And all the notebooks I could carry to this island and away, and all the pencils and pens I could carry to this island and away, and all the days of all the time I have a brain to think, and I will not completely understand nor see the frog, just the frog that the heron ate, even that one small part of the heron's life I cannot know.*

I can try but I cannot know it. And there was some fear in the knowledge but also satisfaction that there could be mystery like that, a mystery that he could spend his life on and not understand. And he sat on the rock and started to think about it, letting his mind float out ahead of him and feeling the sun on his neck when the voice came across the water.

"Hey!" There was a pause, then again: "Hey! How's it going out there?"

Wil stood and walked to the south side of the island. He looked back to the shore where his bike was hidden and saw Susan standing there, waving. He waved at her, then went back for his pack and threw it in the boat and started rowing across the lake to where she waited. It was late afternoon anyway and maybe time to go back. But part of him stayed on the island, a large part, and he thought how nice it would be to stay there overnight, with a small fire by the rock, sleeping under the boat.

HERON

By Wil Neuton

Sometimes the heron isn't there even when he's there.

All tall lines and long lines, he stands in the reeds and grass along the side of the bay and does not curve until he looks down for a frog or minnow, he freezes and holds the stillness for such a long time that even when you're looking at him, looking right at him and you know he is there all gray-metal-shine and beautiful he disappears and isn't there even when he is there.

I tried to paint it in that manner and show the way he can not be there when he is there but of course that is impossible because there would not be a painting of him if he could be painted when he disappears. But he does.

At first I thought of him as he was, the way he stood in the shallows in the reeds, stood for hours as still as the reeds, one leg raised, poised, waiting for a small fish or frog to come close. He is all grace and lines and I tried to move the way he did, show the curve with my body the way he did and that worked some, worked a little. But it was not enough to see him as he is and then I decided that the way to look at him, to look at blue herons with all their beauty, might be to see where they aren't; to look for the shadow of them instead of the body of them.

Then I could see the heron. Then I could see more of the heron than looking directly at him, the way at night you can see more of a thing by looking to the side instead of directly at it. I could see the heron.

I could see the heron in the water at his feet, the reflection of the shadow and the reflection of the bird, caught in the mirror of the water and showing better, showing more detail.

I could see the heron in the wind that came, the small breeze that moved the reeds slightly, a gentle waving, and did not move the heron; the movement showed more of the heron than the stillness did.

I could see the heron in the blue of the sky, in the knowing that he could fly and float on the air.

I could see the heron in the morning sun, making a hole in the gold of the new light.

I could see the heron in all the things the heron was, without seeing the heron at all, and it changed me, made me look at all things that way, made me see in a new way and, finally, made me look at myself in that new way.

Not at what I was, not at what I looked like or could see of myself but at what I wasn't that made me what I was. I saw my shadow, saw myself in the wind and the reeds and the water; saw myself in the morning light, in the gold on my skin, saw myself in my friends, saw myself in Susan, saw myself in the faces of my parents and the way my mother smiled or my father yelled—in all that I wasn't I found myself.

I could see the heron, finally, with every one of his

gray-blue feathers shining on the edge of purple, with his tapered beak and crest and curved-over neck and clean lines and by not looking at the heron I could see me.

At the end, I could see myself in the heron.

8

I never really understood the whole idea of serenity or peace until I saw this guy in a gas station. I was getting some air in my bike tire, and he pulled up to get some gas in a van. When he got out to work the pump, a small dog jumped out of the van and trotted away. Cute little dog. So the guy stopped pumping gas and called, really soft, for the dog to come and get back in the van. But the dog didn't come. The guy called a little harder, kind of walking just in back of the dog, and it still wouldn't come, and so he called a little harder, then a little harder, and pretty soon he was screaming and swearing and chasing this little dog all over the gas station, insane with rage, a wild animal almost frothing at the mouth. And when he was just about to go completely into a state of crackers, the dog looked at him, wagged his tail, and jumped up into the van and sat on the seat while the guy went back and finished pumping gas. I figure the dog had serenity.

—Wil Neuton

SUSAN waited silently until he had the boat up on the shore. Then she helped him turn it over. "I didn't mean for you to go home. I thought maybe if you didn't mind I would come out to the island with you. . . ."

Wil wiped the dirt from the boat off his hands and went to his bike. "I was ready to leave anyway. It's getting kind of late."

She nodded and followed him out on the road, where they started to ride but held the speed down. There were some rain clouds coming, but they were summer soft and several hours away. The rain wouldn't come until after dark, so there was no pressure.

"That was a strange dance," Susan said. She was riding in the right rut and having a little trouble balancing. "Or whatever. I went up along the bank and watched you for a while . . . was it a dance?"

For a moment Wil held back, embarrassed. It never occurred to him that somebody would be watching. He was doing things for himself, he thought—but that wasn't quite right either. He was doing them to try and understand things, to understand the heron, understand how the heron was, how it could be. "It wasn't a dance, or maybe it was sort of—I don't know. I was trying to understand something."

"The heron?"

He looked at her, letting his bike coast. "How did you know that?"

She blew hair back out of her eyes. "It wasn't so hard. I saw the heron fly earlier, and when you did that dance or whatever it was, I thought you looked kind of like the heron. Or maybe not that, but how you thought the heron should look. But they don't call them herons around here—they call them shypokes."

"Shypokes?"

Susan nodded. "Funny name, isn't it? But that's what

they call them. Well, here's my place. You want to come in? See what a milking farm is all about?

Wil stopped and straddled his bike but shook his head. "I have to get home. But maybe . . ."

"Maybe what?"

"I need to go to town tomorrow and buy some stuff. Maybe you'd like to come with me?"

"What time?"

"Early?"

"I'll be at your place at seven, how's that?"

"Fine. We'll bike over to Pinewood and you can show me the sights."

She wheeled down her driveway, waved, and Wil rode the rest of the way home slowly, thinking. If she saw the heron, maybe he was making the heron somehow, maybe he was understanding it and didn't know how he was understanding it; it was just coming through him.

When he turned in the yard, his father was just driving in with the state pickup. Wil waved, put his bike back under the eaves of the house to protect it from the rain, and went in. His father was already in, and his mother was sitting at the kitchen table with a cup of coffee. She had poured a cup for his father, and Wil got a glass of milk.

"Wil . . ."

His mother's voice was what Wil called Grownup-Serious.

"What, Mom?"

She held up the note he'd left that morning. "I just want to know a little more about this island. All of a sudden an island. Out of nowhere, an island. What does it mean?"

56

His father sat at the table, took a sip of coffee, and looked sharply at Wil. "What island?"

"This." His mother handed over the note. "Wil left it this morning. I just want to know about it. How come an island all of a sudden?"

Wil smiled. "It's not all of a sudden. I mentioned it the other night, but I guess you didn't hear me. It's just a small island in a lake up the road. Kind of a neat place. I've been there a couple of times now and sort of camp and look at things. It's not a big deal. . . ." But even as he said it, he knew that it was—in his mind it had become a big deal. He had found something on the island—no, he had found something to look for on the island, or maybe he had found a way to look for all things on the island. "It's not a big deal," he repeated. "I just go there and sit and think and look at the country. See the wildlife."

And they nodded, as he knew they would, because there was nothing wrong in what he had done. Then there was supper, and after that they turned on the television because it was what they did, and there was a show about a car that talked and sang and sometimes danced. It was an awful show, but they left it on as they usually did for background sound, and his mother wrote some letters on a pad in her lap and his father read some magazines about berry farming; and the silly program had the car talking and singing through an hour, and Wil could not stop thinking of the island.

What was it like there at night? What happened in the dark? Was it the same place? When the car show was over, there was another one, about a man made from parts of a computer, and that was worse than the car show because he didn't do anything at all, not even sing or talk much, but just sat around and thought. There was some kind of crime, an espionage thing, and he solved it by sitting and thinking and they would show his face while he was thinking; and when it was time for commercials, they would have somebody wearing a polyester suit selling polka records or organ tapes; when that was on, the rain came and Wil thought of the rock on the island and how it would look in the rain, the soft summer rain.

At one point he took out the notebook and found a blank page and tried to draw how the rock would look in the rain, but it didn't come, and he knew he would have to be there to see it to draw it, to know it.

At eleven they turned off the television and went to bed, and Wil went to sleep thinking still of the island, listening to the rain running off the roof and splashing in the driveway and thinking of the island while sleep came to him, pushed him gently down. And down.

He awakened at six and brushed his teeth and ate a banana with some milk. Susan pulled into the driveway on her bike at almost exactly seven. His parents weren't up yet, so he left a note on the table saying where they were going, and with his pack on his back he followed her out to the road.

The rain had stopped, the sky was blue with spotted white clouds here and there and a warm sun, and there were puddles everywhere. At first they tried to miss them, but then, laughing, they went through and let the water from the wheels come up to the middle of their backs. When they had gone three miles on the gravel-dirt, they hit asphalt, and on the last eight miles into Pinewood the bicycles seemed to float faster than the two of them could pedal, side by side, laughing and talking.

"Pinewood has one of everything," she said, as they went past the town limits sign. "One church, one bar, one grocery store, one dime store, one hardware store, one gas station, one school—this is where we go to school. Next fall. The school has all the grades, from kindergarten through twelfth. One school. For all of us."

"I need some drawing paper. Some paper without lines. And some more notebooks."

"That would be at the one dime store." Susan looked ahead and behind, then crossed over the street and pulled up in front of a store that had a sign proclaiming, IVER'S FIVE AND DIM, with the E missing on DIME, and Wil smiled. He started to lock his bike, but she stopped him. "No need here. You're used to the city. Nobody here locks anything up."

"That's kind of hard to believe."

"But it's true. When the tourists come, they don't believe it either, but that's the way it is around here."

He followed her into the store. It had just opened, and the owner, a large man named Iver Johnson, smiled at Wil. "You must be the new people, come to work the highway. Glad to have you."

Wil nodded and started looking at the shelves. Everything was old and had been there a long time and was dusty, but after a bit he found the paper. There weren't any drawing tablets so he settled for a package of three hundred sheets of typing paper—at least it didn't have lines—and four notebooks. He also bought some felt-tip pens with different ink colors and some plain pencils and a small sharpener. There was also a small water-color set, one of the cheap ones for beginners, and as an afterthought he put in on the counter with the rest of the stuff.

"Going to be doing some writing?" Iver said, but it was just conversation and he didn't expect an answer. Wil dug out some money, the last of his allowance, and paid for what he'd got. There was money left, and he smiled at Susan.

"Can I get you a Coke or something?" *It's so easy,* he thought. *So easy to be with her. Why was I embarrassed around girls before? And why am I not embarrassed around girls now?* "Is there a one place in town for that?"

She smiled and nodded. "Over at the cafe. Come on."

They went outside, and Wil put the paper and materials in his pack and left it on his bike—still a bit uncomfortable with the idea of just leaving things—and they started across the street, actually the highway, to the cafe. When they were just at the edge of the sidewalk, the cafe door opened and a large boy came out. He was a full head taller than Wil, with wide shoulders, and he stopped on the step and towered over Wil.

"You must be the new kid." It was a statement, not a question, and said in a flat tone—on the edge of being insulting. "I'm Ray Bunner." He had not looked at Susan before, but now he swiveled his eyes to her. "What are you doing with him?"

"That's none of your business." Susan bridled. "And never was, Ray Bunner."

He looked back to Wil. "We'll talk about this later."

Oh good, Wil thought—*la, la. I wonder if it takes prisoners or just eats them?* "So what's to talk about?"

"How long you're going to live, for one thing." And

with that he stepped past the two of them and walked across the road to a pickup, which he got in and drove away with much squealing of tires and clouds of dust and smoke.

"That's Ray Bunner," Susan said as they watched him drive away.

"I got that much. Sounds like a nice guy. . . ."

Susan looked at Wil and saw him smiling ruefully. "He isn't. You'll have to fight him later, probably at school."

"Why?"

"Because everybody has to fight Ray. That's how Ray is. Just let him punch you once and go down, and that will be the end of it."

That's for sure, Wil thought. *He'll break every bone in my body with one punch. I'll spend the rest of my life in a wheelchair.* "Maybe we can talk it over . . ."

"I doubt it. He's a real bottom-feeder. He's fifteen and still in the seventh grade, if that gives you an idea. Ray isn't real long on talking things over." Susan shrugged. "But that's for later. Let's get a Coke."

She went up the steps and into the cafe. Wil followed her. Inside it was dark and cool, and several groups of men were sitting at the counter and at tables drinking coffee and eating sweet rolls and pieces of pie. They had been talking, and they all fell silent when Susan and Wil walked in. Once they saw who it was, they went back to talking.

Susan led Wil to the counter. "Hi, Marge," she said to the waitress, a short, chunky older woman. "This is Wil. His dad is the new highway man. We need a couple of Cokes."

Marge nodded and smiled but said nothing and brought

the Cokes. Wil put a dollar on the counter, and she took it to the cash register and brought change—another surprise. Cokes were cheaper here. Everything was different in Pinewood.

"Everything is different here," he said aloud.

"How do you mean?" Susan sipped through her straw.

"You don't lock anything. Food is cheaper. People seem to be more friendly—unless you count the Godzilla we met coming in. And even he's not the same. He's mean but almost civilized about it. Like he's supposed to be mean—I mean, really, peeling out like that in the truck. In the city they don't do that. Tires cost too much. It's just different here—everything."

And the island, he thought. *That, too.* But he didn't say it, not aloud.

They finished their Cokes in silence, and Wil half-listened to the men sitting drinking coffee. They were all farmers, and the night rain had kept them from working in the fields, so they sat and talked about work while they waited for the fields to dry. It had never occurred to Wil that somebody grew the food he ate. He knew it, of course, but he never thought of men who could not get to work because of rain, never thought of men who sat in cafes drinking coffee and talking about wet fields and how the crops looked and how nice the rain was to come just when they needed it. Wil had never thought of farmers, and he listened to them now and tried to remember what they were saying because he wanted to write it in the notebooks, write it and understand it on the island the way he was trying to understand the loons and the heron and the frog and fish . . .

"What's the matter?" Susan interrupted his thinking,

pushing her Coke glass aside. "Your eyes went away."

"Oh. Nothing. Just thinking. Sorry. I was kind of listening to the men talking, and my mind went blank."

"Sometimes," she said, smiling, "sometimes you're kind of weird. Really nice, but weird. Come on, let's go." And she was up and gone, and Wil followed her out the door and across to the bikes and out of town in the noonday sun. He pedaled to catch up to her.

"Hey. Does that offer about coming to your farm still stand?"

She laughed. "Sure. Why?"

"I'd like to know a little more about it," he said. "See how it works." *To know the men in the cafe*, he thought.

"We'll go there now if you like. Have dinner."

"You're on."

Then she set cadence, and he copied her, and they picked up speed and rode through the sun and drying puddles, following their tires.

THE CAFE

By Wil Neuton

We were probably not supposed to listen.

That is, we were allowed to listen to them and nothing they said was secret but they were just talking—the farmers—and although it was all right to hear them we were probably not supposed to listen.

Because they talked of things that were part of their lives, maybe part of how they lived privately. But sitting in the cafe talking with Susan some of what the farmers were came through in what they said, the way music comes through in a song where you don't hear the words so well, but hear the music and know the music better than you wind up knowing the words.

Because I didn't know about farming. Oh, I'd read the stuff in school and heard the things they tell us on TV about how the crops were doing or not doing or how much grain they were going to sell to Russia or China—I knew all that. Or maybe I didn't know it, but I had heard all of that.

I didn't know until Susan and I sat in the cafe and listened to the farmers sitting with their coffee and rolls and heard them talk. It had been raining and they had all their spring planting done and came in to the cafe for morning coffee, as they called it, and I looked at them before I listened to them. Saw their hands all cracked and dirty holding the thick white cups with the steam coming up and taking small sips because they didn't want to drink coffee so much as talk. Talk and talk and eat the rolls with the frosting and jelly centers which they buttered with thick layers of yellow butter, not margarine but butter.

I tried not to stare but their hands were so strong and tight, like the skin was iron on their hands, iron barely able to hold the power in. It seemed their hands were so strong they couldn't hold the cup without breaking it, smashing it; couldn't butter the rolls without tearing them apart and bending the knives and smearing the butter down on the table.

And there was the same power, the same strength in their voices, the rolling way they talked. The same power in their voices as in their hands and their faces.

One man had no hair on top of his head but had a cap covering the bald spot, or almost all of it, and thick hair by his ears that went down into the ears and he smiled so that his teeth were light-white against the sun-dark of his face, white and even, and he said that if he didn't make a crop and it didn't look like he would, if he didn't make a crop this would be his last year—and even if he did make a crop it would be his last year. Just like that. He said it with a smile, a wide smile, and when I looked to see if he was kidding he wasn't. Or maybe he was kidding but it was true and he was smiling at how sad it was that it was true.

Three other men sitting with him nodded, all nodded and had small smiles and one of them said that he had bought a new tractor back when grain prices were all right, and now he would lose that, lose the tractor and maybe part of his farm if he was lucky and how about some more coffee over here, Marge. Tractor gone and maybe part of his farm, his home, and how about some more coffee, Marge.

And Marge poured them coffee, the steam coming up and Susan and I sitting at the counter and I saw that Marge wasn't smiling and Susan wasn't smiling and I wasn't smiling but the farmers at the table were and I didn't understand that. Then I remembered something a teacher had said in world history once—he had stood in front of us and said that all of what man was, all that we had become in all our time and all we would become in all the time we had left, we owed to six inches of topsoil and the fact that it rained when we needed it to rain. Because if we didn't grow food we would all starve. And I thought then that I knew about farming but I didn't and I think now the teacher was wrong.

There has to be six inches of topsoil and rain when we need the rain but that is only part of it and not the biggest part, I think. Because somewhere in there must come the men in the cafe and their strong hands holding the cups without breaking them because when I listened to them I found that I couldn't draw a line between where the soil and rain ended and where they began. They are part of it, part of what the teacher was talking about. We need six inches of topsoil and rain when the rain is supposed to come and the men with the strong hands.

In the cafe.

9.

Everybody is always looking for something for life to be like. One teacher told me once that life was like an onion, and you just kept peeling back layers and never really got to the middle of it. And I thought that was good for a while. But it hit me one day that I didn't want my life to be like an onion. Might as well say life was like garlic. Too strong and stinky. So somebody else told me life was like an Oreo cookie, and you had to eat the hard brown part before you got to the good middle part. Even if you split the cookie and licked the white part off, you paid; you had to lick until your tongue was raw to get it all. That sounded right for a while. Then they came out with the double-stuffed cookies that came apart really easy, and that seemed to make the whole thing wrong; life somehow couldn't be like a double-stuffed Oreo cookie. It would be too easy to throw away the outside and just eat the inside. And then came a whole bunch of things for life to be like—life was like a beach, life was like a treadmill, life was like a carnival, life was like a barrel full of bricks. I had an uncle one time who told me life was like a sewing machine, and no matter what you did you couldn't put the thread in while it was running. Of course he had trouble with drinking so that might not have meant much. I finally figured life isn't like anything. Life is just like life. And it doesn't have a peeling or double stuffing, as far as I can tell.

—Wil Neuton

"No, no, you've got it all wrong." Susan laughed. They were standing at the end of the barn watching the cows come in to be milked. They had spent the afternoon poking around the farm, Wil trying to stay out of the way, asking questions. Now it was five and time to milk—do what Susan called "the chores"—and the cows knew it. They had been out to pasture, and when it came close to five they started to come to the back of the barn, waiting for the door to open. As soon as Susan's brother opened it, they started in, single file, each cow going to its right milking stanchion. A couple butted each other a few times, but after that they went where they belonged and stood to be milked. It was all amazing to Wil—another world again. In one end of the barn there was a compressor room, and pipes ran from it all over the place. The family had milking machines, and they would put the rubber milkers on the cows, and the milk was pulled out and up through a pipe into the bulk tank in the end of the barn, which was kept cool by another compressor system. All automatic. While the cows were being milked, they were fed some ground grain, and each of them had a watering cup; and when they were done, they were released to go back outside and to pasture again.

Slick, Wil thought, *slick as butter*. But that wasn't what he was wrong about; he was wrong about food. "Let me try again," he said. "You eat five times a day?"

"Right."

"But lunch isn't lunch, it's dinner?"

"Right."

"Then what do you call dinner?"

"Supper."

"So. I think I've got it now. But go over it one more time. . . ."

"All right. We have breakfast, then forenoon lunch, which is really coffee and cake or cookies and maybe a lunchmeat sandwich and some pickles; then we work again and stop for the middday meal, which is dinner, which you call lunch, and that's meat and potatoes like we had today; then we work again and stop for afternoon lunch, which is coffee and cake or cookies and maybe a small sandwich and some pickles again, and then we work again—do chores—and after that we're done for the day, and we sit down to supper, which you call dinner, which is meat and potatoes and the whole works. Got it?"

Wil nodded. "What I don't see is how come you aren't all so fat you can't walk."

"I don't know. Except that when we work, we work hard. I guess we burn it off. Josie, dammit, you get along now or we'll make hamburger out of you." Susan had turned to yell at a cow who had finished milking but instead of going outside had tried to butt into another stall and get the food from another cow. Susan grabbed her tail and gave it a mild twist, and Josie headed for the back door at a clumsy trot, her udder slamming against her back legs.

"If you don't swear at them, they don't move right."

Both her mother and father worked at the milking, taking the machine off one cow when it was done and putting it on another, stopping to talk now and then, smiling at Wil when they looked up and saw him: Susan's brother had gone outside and was doing something with machinery—"He's always doing something with machinery"—and it all went so smoothly Wil thought it was almost like a precision machine in itself. The cows would come in, slide into the stanchion, a milker would be put on, and they would get milked and head outside, all in one motion.

"It's amazing," he said, shaking his head. "All amazing. It's a whole thing I never really thought about. A whole new thing to think about, to learn about."

Susan studied him seriously. "You're changing. Just since I met you, you're changing really fast."

"You haven't known me. . . ."

"I know. But just in these few days you're changing all the time, growing somehow. It just shows. Like in the cafe, you sat and listened to the farmers and you kind of . . . kind of glowed with it or something."

It's the frog, he thought. *The heron and the frog and the island and all of it. The island.* But he didn't speak of it. They spent the rest of the evening helping with the milking, and Wil learned how the milk went into the tank, how everything had to be washed several times a day, how the cows were pampered and fed and coddled and even played music to get them to give more milk; how every other day a stainless-steel truck came to pick up milk; how the checks came once a month from the dairy; and through all of it he thought only of the island, wondered what was happening on the island.

When the sun was setting and dusk coming down, he said good-bye to Susan and her parents and biked home. Dinner—supper he thought, smiling—was ready when he got there, and he washed up and slid to the table just as his mother and father sat down.

"How was your day?" Wil's mother asked, ladling

out noodles to be covered with a hamburger sauce. A kind of Stroganoff they had often but which his father said was like something they had in the army. His mother's voice had a kind of tingling edge to it—like glass about to break. Wil's ears perked up. She almost never asked about his day. And when that edge came to her voice, it usually meant trouble. "Did you go to the island?"

Wil shook his head. "I thought I said in the note. I went to town with Susan, then over to her place. They have a dairy farm. Cows and cows and lots of milk."

"And how about your day," she said, looking at his father. "Was it nice?"

Loaded questions, Wil thought, hearing the sudden edge in her voice. *Cobra questions*. But his father missed the edge.

He smiled. "Good. Had a good day. Worked some new road and met a new man. Nice guy named Bunner. Harris Bunner. Funny name but a really nice guy. Helped me figure out where to go. . . ."

That's the way of it, Wil thought. Kids' wars are never grown-up wars, and grown-up wars are never kids' wars. "I met his son. He eats meat and doesn't take prisoners. . . ."

"What do you mean?" his father asked.

"Doesn't anybody want to know what my day was like?" His mother's voices rattled the windows. "Or are we just ignoring it?"

Stunned silence. After a moment Wil said quietly, "What was your day like, Mother?"

"Oh, fine, fine. Up until nine-thirty this morning when the water heater blew up . . ."

"Hmm," Wil's father said, "you know, I thought the house seemed a little damp."

". . . and I had to call Emil Aucht again . . ."

This might not be a good time to bring up the island, Wil thought. He had been thinking of taking camping gear and spending the night out there, but it didn't seem to be stacking up as a good time to talk about it.

". . . and when he went outside for a part, his dog got in the house . . ."

Bob, Wil thought, *I wonder what happened to Bob?*

". . . and the dog started chasing the cat, and Emil started chasing the dog, trying to get it outside, and they went all over the house, up and down, into the basement, with Emil chasing the dog and carrying a can to spit in. Only he didn't hit the can all the time, and it's impossible, just impossible, to find every spot, and some of them were in the kitchen, on the stove, where the food was cooking and some of them . . ."

So, Wil thought, *I wasn't really hungry anyway*. He noticed out of the corner of his eye that his father had put his fork down as well.

". . . were on the walls, and I can't, *can't* boil the whole house. And the cat, the cat was stuck on top of the kitchen window, and the dog, the dog left footprints up inside the kitchen cabinets, and Emil, Emil fell and spilled the can, my God, spilled the can, and you ask, you sit and ask *What kind of day I had*?"

A quiet evening at the Neutons', Wil thought. The silence held, stretched. At length his mother took a fork full of food and put it in her mouth. "Don't worry. I made sure it was all right." She chewed and swallowed, and Wil and his father slowly copied her. "Emil said he would bill us later for the work."

"Good." Wil's father took a bite much the way Wil imagined he would take a bite of a lizard. "So everything is fixed, is it?"

"Except the cat. Bob is in the basement, probably forever." She smiled, all of it blown out now. "You should have seen him, stuck up above the window over the sink. He looked like a hairy spider with whiskers."

I'll go down in the basement and feed him later, Wil thought. *Find him and feed him. Dog like that could cause permanent trauma. Spit him to death.*

After dinner he helped clean the table and do dishes and then rummaged in the boxes in the basement—after he found Bob and gave him some Kitty-Num-Nums, his favorite—and found the backpack and the tent and the old aluminum cookset from his Boy Scout days. He had been a scout when he was twelve for about two weeks, until he found he didn't like the regimented way of doing things, had been a scout just long enough to get the pack and cookset. He took them upstairs and washed the cookset and put it in the pack, added what canned food he could find, and rolled the tent and his sleeping bag and tied them to the bottom of the pack. At the last he put the pads and typing paper and watercolor set and pens in the large pocket in the middle of the pack.

His parents were watching television. Or had the set on. It was some show about either a golf cart that made jokes or a jeep that ate its young—he couldn't be sure from listening—and Wil worked alone in the kitchen. When he had the pack ready, he put it on the back porch and went into the living room and sat.

He coughed. "I guess I told you guys about this island, didn't I?"

Neither of them answered at first. His father was looking at a berry book—Wil could not believe the number of books on berries, whole books written about just berries, books and books about berries and berries—and his mother was knitting. She loved to knit. Finally she paused and looked up. "Yes, dear. What about it?"

"I thought tomorrow I would go and camp there for the night. Or two. Kind of learn a little more about it. Is that okay?"

"Alone?"

"Yes."

"Wil, are you all right?"

Loaded question, he thought. *Cobra question. In her mind how can you be all right and want to spend the night alone on an island? How to answer it?* "I'm fine. It's just that I'm learning things about the island and about myself and I'd like to study it a bit more. . . ." *Kind of lame*, he thought. *Kind of like a crippled duck, that answer.* But he let it stand, or squat.

"What do you think?" She looked to his father. "Isn't this all rather strange for a boy his age? I mean do you think it's normal?"

"Hmmm. I think it's just incredible." He looked up from the book. "Do you realize there is a type of nematode or something like it that has come from China through the Aleutians and can wipe out your berries with some kind of berry blight in just weeks. Big gamble. Even the nematodes are out to get you. I never liked nematodes. Of course the rewards are vast—says it right here. You can grow seven acres of strawberries and virtually retire, or raspberries are even better."

His mother looked at the ceiling, then shrugged and went back to her knitting. "I guess it's all right."

Saved, Wil thought, *by the berries*. And for a second he felt guilty and couldn't for the life of him figure why he should feel guilty about wanting to stay on the island a while.

10.

I used to think that one thing was all it took to solve a lot of problems. I had a friend named Brian who thought that if he could get enough money it would solve everything. He wanted a really good ten-speed. The high-quality racing kind. So he got a job, but that still wasn't enough, and one day a rich uncle came through and felt sorry for him and bought him the bike. Just like that. But things didn't work out. When he got the bike, Brian found out he wanted to compete, but his legs weren't strong enough so he had to buy leg exercisers, and an indoor bike-riding machine and fancy new rims and tubular tires and special bike-riding shorts and hats and gloves, and then it dawned on him that if he was serious about competing, really serious, he would have to have another bike as a backup. . . . He just about went nuts trying to keep ahead of it and finally gave up. We talked about it and decided things worked just the opposite—it took lots of solutions to solve just one problem. There wasn't a single solution to anything. Which made it really hard to do math for a while. . . .

—Wil Neuton

Aɴᴏᴛʜᴇʀ dawn. Summer light filtering in through the screen cut across his face and awakened Wil, and he rolled out, put his feet down, and stood. *I never used to get up early*, he thought—*hated it. Slept in all the time*.

He cleaned, brushed his teeth, and put the brush in his pack. As an afterthought he found some more cans of food—stew and meat and fruit of various kinds—and put them in around the notebooks and drawing pads. In the bathroom he found a bottle of insect repellent, and he put it in a side pocket of the pack. His parents were still sound asleep so he left yet another note:

Going to the island on Sucker Lake to camp. See you in a day or two. We talked about it last night.
                                        Love, me.

Just in case they forgot about it, he thought. *Cover my tracks*. He tiptoed into the basement, where it still smelled hot and damp, and put down a large bowl of Kitty-Num-Nums for Bob, who was in back of the heating system making low growls. "It'll be all right," Wil whispered to him. "Come up in a day or two and give it another try. Maybe the dog will swallow his tongue and choke."

Upstairs he had a quick bowl of cereal, rinsed the bowl and spoon and left them in the sink, picked up the pack, which was surprisingly heavy, and let himself quietly through the front door. His bike seat had morning dew all over it—sloppy wet—and he wiped it as best he could with the tail of his T-shirt as he wheeled the bike out to the road. Once he was lined up right, he threw a leg over and, with the weight of the pack on his back pushing him off, nearly pitched into the ditch. It took him several tries to get going, and once he was up to speed he had to fight the extra weight on his back, which flopped his balance all over the place. But he held it, and inside of a half mile he had it tamed.

He couldn't go fast, but it wasn't a morning for speed. There were clouds forming, and they would bring another light rain. They were far off, though, and he would make the island before they came. Once he got the tent up, it wouldn't matter. He met the milk truck about halfway to Sucker Lake and pulled off to let him go by, and the driver waved.

The rest of the ride to the island there were no other cars, and he pulled up next to the boat and gratefully shed the pack. It was an unnatural way to carry a heavy load, leaning forward on the handlebars, and he straightened and stretched and rubbed his shoulders where the straps had cut.

A blue heron got up near the boat, but it was smaller than the one he had seen before and flew the opposite way from the island. Standing still and breathing evenly, he watched it fly until it was out of sight; then he turned the boat over and dropped his pack in the bow. It took five more minutes to hide his bike, farther back into the brush than before because he would be gone for a time. He wove branches over it until he couldn't see it from five feet away, then skidded the boat out into the water and hopped in.

He backed around, sitting facing the bow, and rowed toward the island.

It was different now, he thought. It almost felt as if he were coming home. Coming home. *And what a home*, he thought, *what a home for me*. The island lay in the morning like a painting, sitting, almost floating on the water. There was a small breeze making ripples, so there was no reflection, but the island was framed by clouds in the northwest, set into the clouds like part of the sky, and he wanted to paint it, wanted to try to paint it. But this was not the time; he had to get out there and set up the tent and get squared away. Then he could come back.

He set to the oars again, going around the right end of the island. The loons got up, but they knew the boat and landed inside of fifty yards and watched him with a kind of aloof curiosity as he rounded the table rock and rowed the boat to the small beach. Jumping out, he pulled the boat well up onto the sand. Then he studied the way it lay, changed his mind, pushed the boat out and, wading alongside, horsed it ten feet or so down the beach and pulled the boat back up.

Now the boat was on the end of a small depression in the sand, and Wil worked it sideways, lifting first the bow and then the stern, until he had it where he wanted it. Finally he took the pack out, set it on the ground off to the side, and heaved the boat over until it was upside down. In this way the boat formed a wall on one side of the dip in the beach. Again he studied it, frowned, and then smiled. *It could be a porch*, he thought; *the boat could be a porch*.

He went up the beach to where the wind had driven a large pile of driftwood, found two pieces that were dry and stout, about two feet long, and brought them back to the boat. Using his shoulders and back he lifted one side of the boat and spaced the two pieces of drift-wood along the side to form two braces that held up the side of the boat and made a lean-to. Wil kicked at the boat two or three times, and when it was obvious that it was solid, he crawled under it and found a fairly large, cozy room. He smoothed the sand with his hands, threw out a few small sticks and some sharp rocks, then scrabbled out and dragged his pack under the boat. It was as good a shelter as the tent, waterproof and stout. The mosquitoes found him, but he doped up with repellent and they left him largely alone.

It took another twenty minutes to make a fire pit with stones near the side of the boat and another half hour to gather driftwood and break it into smaller pieces to put under the boat to keep dry when the rain came. And when he was finished, he stood and looked at what he had done.

"Where I will be . . ." he said aloud—perhaps to the loons. "Where I will live."

And now a kind of pressure came into his mind, something that told him he should get to work although he did not know what kind of work yet and he did not understand it, found it to be unsettling, and decided that first he would stop everything. Just stop it all. And think gently, meditate.

Wil had talked to people who did karate and other martial arts, and while he did not like the concept of fighting, they talked much of finding peace in their minds and using meditation to do it, thinking themselves blank. Lots of kids in Madison had started it, some in earnest, some just copying what they had seen in films. But Wil had not tried it.

He went out on the flat rock and stood in the middle,

facing the water, his arms at his sides, everything relaxed, and tried to make his mind peaceful.

Nothing.

He felt no different. The more he tried to make himself relax mentally, the less anything happened. Then he remembered what one of the boys who had taken the karate training told him. He had said that you had to try to think of nothing.

But really nothing. "Think of nothing, blankness, make your mind blank," he had said. And Wil tried this now, tried to think of nothing, not a single thing, and at the outset it didn't work. Some thought always crept in. So he tried thinking of things that meant nothing—flat grayness, bright light, making himself mentally visualize the blankness of a flat gray fog with nothing to see in it—and in time, in ten minutes, another ten, a change started to happen.

He did not know how, but his mind started to go blank, and he was thinking of nothing; with his eyes closed and his arms hanging loosely he thought of nothing, a relaxing nothing, a wonderful, peaceful blankness that was the most thoroughly resting thing he had ever felt.

And in the middle of it, in the middle of the peace of it, when his whole being, all that he thought, was gentled and open and peaceful, one of the young loons made a young sound, a tiny sound on the water, and it carried into his thoughts and filled him. Not just the sound of it, but all of what the loon could be filled him, and he stood for a time—he could not know the time now—stood for perhaps a long time, his mind at peace, his eyes closed, taking all things into his thoughts. Not just all the sounds but things from before as well; small things, pretty thoughts—his grandmother cooking once, making rolls for dinner and talking while she did it, laughing while she talked and cooked. He could not remember the dinner, but suddenly all that his grandmother had been to him was in his mind, in his thoughts.

She was there, with the gray hair coming loose from the bun, and telling him stories about when she was a girl up in Minnesota before they moved down to Wisconsin, pushing the hair back and getting flour on her cheek, and all of it came into his mind, his peace. She was there when he used to visit her in the summers, making him cookies and fresh bread with the smells that were so incredible they made his mouth water thinking of them—thinking of them. She was there in his mind. And he was there, the spirit of what he had been was there, a small boy running and running and making a fuss and bother of things while she cooked, clambering into the kitchen to show her something to make her smile and out and in again. All of it in his mind, in the peace and settled thoughts of how he had come to be standing on the rock.

In time, in a time he did not know, his eyes opened, and he was still there, still on the island looking out across the lagoon where the three loons swam. He did not know how long he had stood that way, thinking, meditating, but his grandmother was still fresh, still alive in his thoughts.

"So strange," he whispered. "So strange to find her here . . ." *Alone on an island,* he thought, *the first time I meditate my grandmother happens to me.* "So strange."

Then he turned and went to the boat to get his notebook and write about his grandmother while it was still fresh.

GRANDMOTHER

By Wil Neuton

It is not an easy thing to write about my grandmother because she is dead, and death for some reason makes it hard to think about her. I do not know
why this has to be. When she was alive I hardly
thought of her at all except when we would go to see
her, and now that she is dead it is unpleasant to
think of her because the memory is sad. Or the
thoughts that come from the memory are sad—not
the memory itself.

But there is so much to know about her, to feel
about her, to think about her that even though it is
difficult I should do it, and so I will.

My grandmother.

She lived in a small town called Solway in southern Wisconsin. Her house was on the outside edge of
town near a creek or small river and we would visit
her once a year, in summer. When my parents got
ready to go home after the day I would carry on and
make whining noises to stay with her for a "few
days" which usually became a week and they would
let me stay. Twice more in the year we would see
her, at Thanksgiving and at Christmas. But both
those times she came to visit us and that wasn't the
same as going to her house.

She was small and thin and had very tiny wrists.

They were thin and hard and her hands were thin and hard and she crocheted hour after hour with thin wrists and large knuckles which I asked her about once and learned they were from arthritis. When I asked her it was in the evening and we had been sitting at the table eating apple pie which she had made for me, and drinking thick milk which she had bought from a farm on the outside of town. I asked her about her thin wrists and how her knuckles seemed large and wished right away I hadn't done it because I could see that it hurt her.

She hid her hands for a bit and I have no excuse except that I was young then, only six, and still basically stupid. But in a moment her hands came out again and she told me to wait at the table and she went into the small bedroom with the feather bed and brought out an old photo album. And oh, she showed me pictures I had never seen before—pictures of times I didn't know and people I didn't know and places I didn't know and all of them were her. They were her life.

We sat that time with the photo album and drank milk and she showed me all of her life, pointing with the thin wrists and the large knuckles.

First there was an old man carrying an armload of wood split for a stove and next to him was a small girl, a tiny girl with a dirty dress. It was her. The dress was small and went out at the bottom and looked to be covered with mud or streaks of charcoal and the face was round with tiny eyes, tiny slits of eyes in fat little cheeks that smiled as the girl looked at the camera.

She told me it was an early picture of her with her father, which made him my great-grandfather so I studied the picture closely. I could see that he was a tall, slabby shouldered man, but the picture was very old and fuzzy so I couldn't tell much else about him.

The girl showed better, her face was in the light and you could almost but not quite see the freckles. When I looked from the picture to Grandmother's face and back again I could see it—I could see the little girl in her. It was in her eyes and in her cheeks and some of the freckles and when she smiled I knew it was her and for that time she was young. For that time in my mind she was young.

Then she turned the page and there were other pictures, pictures of farm houses and ponies and log barns. They were all black and white photos, with gray edges, glued on the black felt paper—places she lived, things she lived. We sat there and looked at the pictures and I tried to understand how she had lived but could only guess, really.

Then another picture, this time an older girl, a young woman. She stood in a long dress with a bunch of ruffles in the back and a full front. Now her hair was long and down her back, combed in long, straight lines and she told me the picture was taken the day she graduated from high school in Norway. She was beautiful then, beautiful in the way she stood and beautiful in the way her hair framed her face and neck and shoulders and fell down her front and the side. It was all in waves, slow waves of hair, and I asked her about it, not about the beauty of the young woman in the picture but about how she had done her hair so beautifully, how it could have been done.

She told me that she used to spend hours and hours curling it, working it. She had to heat an iron, a thing called a curling iron, on a wood stove and when it was hot enough but not so hot it would burn her hair she would curl one, two, perhaps three waves and then the iron would be too cool and she would have to reheat it. Sometimes it took all night, waving and curling and reheating the iron and waving and curling. When it was done she told me that it would only last a few days, a week at the most if the weather stayed dry and then the waves, the falling waves, would be gone, "hung out," she said, hung out and gone. "Then it was all to do over." She sighed when she said that. "Then it was all to do over and over and that was what it was like to have hair like that, hair to fall down your back in waves like a waterfall when I was a young woman, a young lady," she said.

I thought about that for a while, thought about the beauty that she had then in the picture and now in her eyes and I asked her why, why she would spend all those nights and nights heating the irons on the wood stove. And there came such a smile into her eyes, such a smile, and she said it was because, finally, of Clarence. "It was because of Clarence who came for me one night when I was in a white dress, a new white dress with stitches so tight it was as if it was all of a cloth."

Stitches she said she had done herself when she made the white dress from a pattern from Sears that came through the mail; stitches she sewed on long winter nights to make a dress to wear to the church social and to wear again when Clarence came for her on a soft summer night. That was why she spent the hours with the curling iron. Because Clarence came in a suit so tight he looked like a stove pipe, a tall hard suit, and a stiff back and so shy he almost couldn't stand in the light.

"Clarence," she said, and her eyes had that beauty again, the soft look. "He came for me, to ask for me," she said, "and he stood stiff and raw and shy that way and I had my hair all down my back and the white dress, just like in the picture, and he spoke in those soft ways to my father and mother about his farm, which he was going to own, and how he felt about farming and livestock and how the market for oats was down but the market for wheat was going up a little.

"He spoke of all those things and never spoke of me, never spoke of me," she said, "but I knew he was there to speak for me and finally he asked if I could go with him for a ride. I was sixteen, sixteen come a lady, as my mother, your great-grandmother, used to say, I was sixteen come a lady and Clarence became your grandfather that you never met. He was young and raw then," she said, "but clean to grow and I loved him so I thought my heart would burst with it and that's why I spent the time to curl my hair," she said.

There were soft tears in her eyes and her finger, her thin finger with the joints so thick, touched the picture, the gray-white picture of the beautiful young girl, like she was trying to touch the memory, like she was trying to touch Clarence. Oh my grandmother, I thought, oh my grandmother, I do not know you and I thought I did but I do not know you because I did not know this about you. I saw the thin wrists and the large knuckles and the crocheting and did not know or think of Clarence and the hair that went down like a waterfall.

She turned the page then to a new place in the album and I saw a woman on a farm. Older now, she was, with her hair up and shorter and you could see the work on the woman. She was in the back yard of a farm house, standing there, with the sun on her dress, a dark dress now, not white but perhaps a color that didn't show on the old black and white photograph. It could have been red. She stood with one hand on her hip in the picture and in back of her, next to the house, there was a clothesline with all sorts of sheets and white cloth hanging, a slash of white that framed her. She looked strong and in the arm on her waist you could see cords of muscles. A short piece of hair hung down in her eyes, just a short piece.

When I saw the picture it made me feel that I should reach over and push the hair out of her eyes.

That's the way it hung down. And now when she touched the picture and I looked up at her eyes they still had the beauty, but more, too—they showed some kind of strength I didn't understand and still don't understand. Not power so much as strength, or maybe gentle strength—the kind of strength a tree might have. She smiled at the picture, touching it and said how she was a mother three times when the picture was taken, three times and all daughters, strapping daughters with long legs and laughter and one of them was my mother, she said.

"Three daughters," she told me, and there were tears down her face as she spoke and I couldn't know why she had the tears and so I asked her, why, why having three daughters then and being strong made her cry. For a time I didn't think she was going to answer me and I thought I had hurt her again, but then she smiled and said that it was sad in the way that happy things are sad. The daughters had health and strength and had found good lives, all that came from her, came from when she was standing in the sun in the yard, the daughters passed from her and took from her and it was happy but sad, too. She was then a woman, she said to me, sitting and looking at the album.

She turned the page again, two pages, skipping one, but I got my finger in between and turned it back and there was a young man now, with blond hair and blue eyes and standing in a uniform but I did not know him.

She looked at the picture briefly and turned it under again but not before I saw a tearing thing in her eye, a great and sad and tearing thing that was so powerful it frightened me. And I asked her about it but she said something about a neighbor man, a young man she knew, who did not come back from the war.

"The damned war," she said, "the damned war." But it was not her son, she had not had a son because I had no uncles on her side, only on Dad's side, and she did not act like the man had been related to her. But her voice got tight and she said they had not even gotten the body back, not even that and she made a sound in her throat, a sound like a growl, not a grandmother sound but a woman sound, a mad woman sound and we turned the page once more and that was gone, the thing with the young man was gone except from her eyes, the tough woman eyes, the angry eyes that still had beauty.

She turned page after page and I saw all of her life in slices, each page one or two pictures, each page a slice. There were pictures of her standing by an old car, other pictures by a team of horses or a buggy or a tractor or at a picnic. And each picture is burned into me even though it was years ago when we sat and looked at the album because I had told her she had ugly hands.

And there is that about it, I guess, there is that good about it the way some good can come from something bad. I learned something about her that I would not have known if I had not made her cry with my stupidity. But it is hard now.

It is hard to write of her when she is gone and sometimes when I sit and think of her, to learn of her, I feel the tearing thing she must have felt when we saw the picture of the young man who had been a neighbor and perhaps a bit more; I feel that tearing thing and probably have the same look or something like that look in my eye.

11.

Another thing I've had to be careful about is the old sayings that are supposed to work so well. Like "a stitch in time saves nine," or "a rolling stone gathers no moss." They are from the old days and can get kind of scary if you try to apply them to modern times. The one that got me to thinking was "a penny saved is a penny earned." I worked on that for a while and thought saving might be the way to go. I mean, hardly anybody sews anymore, and the business of rolling a stone—well, it doesn't scan and that's it. Saving a penny is about the same. Joe Hodges and I did some research and found that if you try to save a penny now, what with inflation and the expense of moving it and handling it to get it into a bank where it can earn interest, by the time you get the penny saved it would actually cost you several cents. Of course the saying could be applied to larger amounts, but as Joe Hodges puts it, "The machine works just the same, just the same."

—Wil Neuton

HE worked all the rest of the day on the piece about his grandmother, and when he had said some of the things he wanted to say and it seemed to be right, he put the notebook aside and ate a cold can of beef stew. It was too much for him, too salty and too cold, with congealed bits of fat that were not very appetizing. When he was done, there was still some stew in the bottom of the can, and he was planning to bury it until he noticed a mound in the trees just up from the beach. He found it to be an anthill.

He placed the can gently on its side at the bottom of the mound so that the leftover stew made a puddle in the bottom and then settled back to watch. When he was a small boy, he used to put a piece of candy down by the little ant mounds in the cracks of the sidewalks and watch the ants come out for the candy. Those had been small red ants and they had seemed for the most part to spend all of their time running madly in circles—some of them hitting the candy, some of them missing.

But in the mound on the island there were large black ants, some of them strangely red and black. They had huge mandibles which, when they bit—as Wil found later—could take out a respectable chunk of meat. For a time they did nothing, seemed to ignore the can and the stew. Ants went up and down the hill, foraging. But as Wil watched, some ants—he thought of them later as scout ants—happened across the can and the stew, and each took a tiny scrap away in his jaws.

Again, for some time—ten or fifteen minutes, perhaps half an hour—there was no difference in the anthill. Some other individual ants came across the can and took a bit of stew, but they were just random hits by the lucky ones. The sun beat down on Wil's neck, and there was, after some time, the smallest nudge at the back of his mind that he might be too old to sit and watch an anthill anymore, maybe people grew out of sitting and watching ants. But it passed, passed with the interest in what was happening. Just as he thought nothing further would come of the stew, a solid mass of ants—three or four hundred, as near as he could guess—came boiling out of the side of the mound near the top, through the sand and pine needles, boiling out with deep intent; and when they were halfway down the mound, another mass came out, more this time, and still more, until a regular stream of ants went from the top side of the mound down to the stew can and back up and into the mound.

The scouts had brought word, he thought. They had told their story. They had done their dance in the small dark rooms for the other ants, perhaps the way bees were supposed to dance to tell of the direction to honey and how far it was. The ants had told, and the mass of them had come. And while he watched, bitten now and then by soldier ants that climbed his ankles above his tennis shoes, they cleaned it out, scoured the can until there was nothing but a small stain in the bottom.

All of the stew gone in less than an hour. Clean and gone. The bits of fat and potato and carrots, even the liquid of the gravy, cleaned and gone; conveyed below ground as if a conveyor belt had been running. Soon the ants were all but gone, a few worker ants cleaning up the mound, the scouts and foragers working out around the mound area in the hope of perhaps finding another empty stew can.

He could only guess what the stew was for; maybe stored for winter food, perhaps carried into the mound to feed the young, or the queen. He had seen a show on television once, on public television, about an ant mound in Africa, and he supposed that ants were like people seemed to be, much the same the world over. The African ants had a truly sophisticated society, with workers, a queen to reproduce young, soldier ants to fight for the anthill when it was invaded, and some just to clean up the place while others brought food in for the queen. Everything was ordered and controlled.

If these ants were the same, they would have carried the food into rooms in the lower part of the mound, below earth, where it would be stored for future use in special storage chambers. Wil closed his eyes and thought of the small rooms, the food stored, the order of it all; he imagined how they would look down underground, how they worked to keep the tunnels cleared, what it was like to be invaded. Once, when he was young and looking for some firewood with his grandmother, he had come across an anthill and had kicked the top of it with a toe, watched the ants scurrying, trying to re-build. *The ultimate invasion*, he thought, *having your house kicked apart by some kid*.

He picked up the empty can and stood, almost falling over backward with the stiffness in his legs. Both feet had gone to sleep, and he took staggering steps back down the beach to the campsite. It was still afternoon but getting late, and he had a small problem: he was thirsty. He thought of boiling lake water, which would have been good enough, or just drinking lake water plain—he didn't know if that was dangerous or not—but decided to take a turn around the island first.

It didn't take long. Still carrying the can, he walked along the beach and rounded the end past the flat rock, then circled the rocky shore to the south side of the island—the outside of the U—until he had come around the other end and was starting back into the bay area.

Here he had some luck. All he had seen until then were trees and willows, but in some sand and rocks on the west end of the island he found a seeping spring trickling water down into the sand. He kneeled and used the can to scoop out a depression in the sand and rocks, and in no time it was full of clear water from the spring. He rinsed the can and let it settle again, then took some and drank it. The water was cool and good, although it had a faint metal taste which Wil guessed came from its passage through all the rocks and sand; he drank another half a stew can full.

I have it all now, he thought—*all I need.*

He rinsed the stew can one more time and walked back to the boat. He wanted to try to paint the ants and the mound and some of his grandmother before the evening came, and the only time he had ever painted with watercolors was when he was small, in grade school, and he couldn't remember what it had been like to use them. *A mess*, he thought—like when they turned him loose with finger paints and he had made a "flower," which looked more like a dying snake, and he had brought it home to his mother. But he had seen watercolors done by artists that were truly beautiful, and so he knew it could be done. *Maybe not by me*, he thought, *but it can be done.*

At the boat he pulled out his pack and rummaged in it until he found the watercolor set. It had three brushes, three different sizes, and he took them out and studied the metal paint box. On the back, in small print, were some instructions with illustrations, clearly done in Japan, he decided, smiling.

"It is necessary first to take the color from the paint

box," he read aloud, "and deposit color on paper before a painting can be constructed."

Right, he thought. *I agree with that.* He read on. "Find some water in small amounts to be used for mixing."

Wil went down to the lake and put a little water in the stew can and carried it carefully back to the campsite. "All right," he said aloud. "I'm ready to paint."

"In the box," he read, "are basically twelve colors. Mixing from them it is possible to make all the colors there are. It is necessary to make an experiment with the blending of the colors to find the right shades. Mix the colors in the depressions in the lid."

There were two drawings showing a hand with a brush taking color from one of the little color pots and mixing it with another color in the dented places in the metal lid. He pulled out a piece of typing paper and, using the notebook as a back, settled in the sand on his haunches. Then he dribbled a bit of water in the blue color pot, rubbed the brush in, and painted a bit of blue on the paper.

It was pale, too pale to be the sky, far too pale to be the lake. But he could make it darker by repeated applications, and on the fourth layer he had a color not too far from the sky. A gentle blue, an alive blue. Then he added still more blue, and a touch of gray because he thought that might help, and he came up with a slate blue that might be the color of the lake in the wind, when the water took on the slatey color of wave and wind action.

And then red, yellow, all the colors—a dab here mixed with a dab there, a wipe over another wipe, watching the colors change, grow, become more or become less;

sheet after sheet of paper to find the way the colors work with each other to make new colors—and some of the lessons from his art classes in the fifth grade came back, and he covered more paper with the swatches of color, the wipes and spots blending and coming apart until he thought he had a handle on it.

Not to be good, perhaps. Perhaps never to be good. But to make the colors right for what he saw, and the picture right, to help him understand what was happening with the things he wanted to study, to learn from. He tried a painting of the anthill, tried to make the sand and pine needle color and the light from the sun down on the hill, the black-blurred color of the stream of ants coming down the side to the stew can.

Part of it worked. The hill looked too flat, but the stream of ants came alive for him, and he started to throw it aside to do another one but shook his head. "Wait . . . wait . . . wait . . ."

It was light. He had to have light on the mound to make it come out of the paper at him, to make it into an anthill and not a flat cone on paper. Light had to be there as well. Not just color, not just the mixed colors, but the light had to be there to give the colors dimension. Without the light there was nothing. It had to be there, coming from the sun, and the light was . . . was what? Yellow? No. Not this way. It was the absence of color perhaps. *Try it. Try it.*

He was excited now. Discovering the light made him almost thrum with the feeling that the painting could come alive. He dabbed the end of his T-shirt in the water and used it to gently wipe two bands of light down onto the anthill from the right. Where the light hit the hill he repainted to make the colors brighter, and there it was, there it was for him.

The anthill almost jumped off the paper into his brain. He could see it the way it had happened, see the ants taking the stew, smell the rich formic-acid metal taste on his tongue that came when they bit him, feel the sun on his back again as he had while he squatted and watched them.

To paint, he thought. *Just to paint like this and see these things and make them come alive on the paper!* It was strange, so strange, but all there was in a way. To paint and write in the notebook and see and feel and learn and know—to know.

He put the brush in the stew can of water, swished it around to clean it and put it away. Then he took out the notebook and the pencil and wrote:

To paint.

   To write.

      To know.

         To be.

He studied the words for a time, as he did the painting. But it was evening now, and the mosquitoes were getting worse. He redoped himself with repellent and got ready to spend the night. There would be time for more study and work tomorrow, more painting, more writing tomorrow.

It was late, and he worked at getting a fire laid and started.

12.

Blame is a funny thing. The whole idea of blame. If you didn't have blame, nobody could do anything wrong, is the way I look at it. It's even kind of a dumb-sounding word—blame. Sounds like some silly explosion or something—blame, blame. When I was twelve we had a teacher for a while who was really into lists. He had us making lists of everything, trying to show how statistics worked: How many times we ate a certain kind of cereal for breakfast, how many times we bent over to tie our shoes, how many times we went to the bathroom in a week—which made us all wonder about Bradley Halstead when he totaled out at 74 times. But this teacher was crazy for lists for about nine weeks and had us running around keeping track of everything. So I decided to keep a list of the number of times I got blamed for things in a week. Not just blamed incorrectly but even when I did do something wrong—all the times I got blamed. In one week it came up to 32 times I was blamed for things—everything from not taking out the garbage (which was true because I forgot) to losing my lunch money for the week (not true; it went through the washer and didn't make it). Thirty-two times. It was really depressing, and on the last day of the week I was feeling sorry for myself, and I decided to sit down and tell my folks about it. So I laid the whole thing out, and when I got done I leaned back and waited because I figured I had been *wronged. They thought about it for a few minutes, and my dad looked at me and said, "It's all your fault, isn't it—for keeping track of it? You shouldn't keep track of it." And I thought: 33. Blamed again. You can't win with lists.*

—Wil Neuton

Wil awakened instantly, completely lost. Under the boat, the sand warm around him, he forgot for a time where he was and could not join things in his mind. Dark above, dark and curved, light out to the side, the ashes of a fire—nothing made sense.

Then it came to him, and he rolled sideways out of his bag, which was and had been unzipped all night, covering him loosely to keep the worst of the mosquitoes out. It was late. The sun was full up and hot, and the sky was clear. During the night it had rained lightly, coming later than he had originally thought it would, and he could see dappled marks in the sand where the drops had hit.

Rain tracks, he thought. *Rain tracks. Another thought for the notebook. But later, later.*

He found his toothbrush in the pocket of his pack and took the stew can and the brush over to the spring, where he brushed without toothpaste, rinsed, and rubbed fresh water on his face and in his hair. Then he stood, dripping, and looked at the lake and smiled. He had the whole lake. All of it. Why just wash his face?

Back at the boat he quickly shrugged out of his T-shirt and shorts and underwear and ran into the water. It was cold, rich and cold, splashing up on him from his feet, and when it was just over his knees he threw himself forward in a shallow dive and held his breath until his forward motion had stopped. Then he raised his head, reached down with a tentative foot and found the bottom so he could stand about chest deep. He looked around and was surprised to see the loons still there, although farther out now, almost out of the bay. They were getting used to his being there, and seeing them made him feel more and more a part of the lake, part of the island.

He kicked off and in an easy crawl made a half circle around the bay, letting his muscles stretch out the night kinks from sleeping on the ground. When he got back to where it was shallow, he stood and walked out of the water. He used the edge of his hand to wipe much of the water off—the way you use a squeegee to wipe a window—then went to the square rock and stood, turning slowly to let the sun reach all the moisture.

When he was dry, he stood still, hands at his side, sun on his right shoulder, and tried to let his mind go blank, to meditate.

Sun heat, he thought, *sun heat and no thoughts—let there be no thoughts.* He closed his eyes, blanked his mind, felt thoughts of other things creep in, blanked it again, and suddenly he was inside his mind; just suddenly he was there in the same gentle blankness as before, the waiting blankness that last time had brought his grandmother and this time brought nothing, nothing for a time, a time that did not matter.

Then it started. Into the empty place came the sudden picture of a middle-aged Chinese man he had seen on a public television show about China. The man had been doing some kind of exercise. The name didn't come. Twai-chan or something. But the movements came. A mixture of dance and martial arts, of grace and defense, a movement of solidity and of reaching. All of it flowed through Wil's mind as he stood in the sun, and when the image was gone, his eyes opened and he realized that he was doing the movements, had been doing them while he was meditating.

His arms out to the side, then to the front, hands curving over and down, legs going forward, then back in the classic defense pose, hands circling each other. He worked to get grace into the movement, more dance and less martial arts, worked to find the grace in his body. If in one of the circular movements he felt a strain in his arms, he would reach farther next time, make more of a curve, exaggerate the motion still further, stretching and reaching until he felt the sinews pull in his arms and legs, until he felt the muscles almost hurt from the pull.

It was not right yet, the dance, the movement. Only exercise. But he thought that when he got it to be more, when he could reach more and stretch more in the sun, nude on the rock, he could turn his body into anything, the way words in the notebook or paint on the paper could become anything if he could do them well enough. He could become the heron flying, reaching from the water up into the sky perhaps, or even the frog or the grace of the loons diving, rolling, swooping as they must in the water.

He could be all of it if he could make his body work right. All because of the middle-aged Chinese man, all because he had emptied his mind.

He worked for half the morning, reaching, pulling, exercising, worked until he was shining in sweat and the sun was almost directly overhead. Then a dive into the water, shallow to avoid the bottom, another short swim and out and up to the boat. He pulled his shorts on and shrugged into his T-shirt. He was hungry, had not eaten since the bit of cold stew he had shared with the ants—but food did not seem terribly important to him, which did not make sense. He loved to eat, but it had just somehow become secondary.

Just a fuel, he thought. *The way gasoline goes into a car. I just burn it.* He dug in the pack and found a can of beans and molasses and opened them and ate them cold with a spoon, working around the hunk of pork fat in the middle. When the beans were gone, he went to the spring and got a drink, then gave the pork fat to the ants and went back to the boat.

Wil looked up at the sun and saw that there was plenty of afternoon left. He wanted to study a frog and know more about frogs because he did not understand frogs. There were many things he did not understand.

The night before he had lain looking at the fire, propped on one elbow with his sleeping bag open, and he realized that it was the first time he had ever spent a night out alone. He had camped a few times, back in Madison, but always he had been with at least one other boy, and there had always been somebody to talk to. Now he was alone, the frog's song still with him. He lay watching the flames burn down, letting his mind tumble in on itself, and he had a thought-picture of his life, a series of thought-pictures of his life, which passed through his mind like a fast-paced slide show.

Pictures in the flames . . .

A dog they had owned once, lived with once. Fat dog named Fred that loved to swim. A picture of a stick going out through the air over a pond outside of Madison and Fred jumping in to swim-float to the stick and bring it back. *Snap*, the stick hitting the water; *snap*, Fred jumping off the bank; *snap*, laughing as the water splashed on Wil and Bob Stanton.

Fred later hit by a car. That picture, too. His shape on the side of the road, broken and dead and gone; all of the waters and sticks and laughter gone with the going of Fred.

They had to be written or painted, the pictures of Fred, the story of Fred and the stick in the air and the splashing water flying up into the light. . . .

Sitting in a seaplane next to a dock when he was a young boy, not over six, perhaps just six and it was his birthday. His father had rented an hour in a seaplane at the lake to take them up and fly around as a present for him. Scared, so scared he couldn't blink his eyes, and afraid that he would wet, and the pilot strapping him into the small front seat right in back of the copilot's wheel. And the noise—oh, the noise—as the pilot pushed the throttle forward and the plane roared across the waves, the floats skipping and bouncing higher and higher until the plane finally rose into the air, wobbling and rattling with age—he learned later it was almost fifty years old—to plod around the sky over the lake. He had turned in the seat once when they were high over the small roads and ponds and seen his father with a fixed grin on his face, his hands white and gripping each other in his lap; and he knew now that his father was and had always been terrified of heights, of flying, and that he had overcome the fear to take Wil up in the plane, had somehow overcome the fear for that long. . . .

It was to know, to know things that he had come to

the island and would stay at the island, to know as much as he could about good things and bad things, to see into them and know them. It was like a hunger in him as he stared at flames and went to sleep or possibly not to sleep so much as changed his state and slipped down into rest under the boat, to know nothing until the new light brought him up again.

13.

I used to always have trouble with jokes. Telling jokes, under-standing jokes, laughing at the wrong places when other people tell jokes, not knowing when somebody is telling a joke or not knowing when somebody is playing a joke on me—they just didn't work for me. I could laugh at things that were funny. Like when Niles Strand got on the football bus by mistake in the dark, thinking he was on the band bus, and said to the guy sitting next to him that all jocks were stupid, and the guy next to him was the center, who bit the tops off of pop cans and who was going to fix it so Niles would have to have his trumpet sur-gically removed from his throat; and Niles ran over the driver getting off the bus and had to live for two months in the school running from class to class wearing a black raincoat and shades to stay alive—now that was funny. All of it. But I never used to understand about jokes. I kept trying to tell jokes but always blew it. Finally I tried telling the famous joke about how it couldn't have been Santa Claus because Santa Claus didn't ex-ist, and, as might be expected, I told it to my little cousin Jim who was the only eleven-year-old left in the world who believed in Santa Claus—either because he's really dumb or really smart (he always gets lots of presents)—and that was the end of it. I just decided I would never know about jokes. But after a time I realized that the way I handled jokes was a joke. When I

107

laughed at the wrong places in jokes, that became a joke for the people who were telling me the joke and made a new joke because they laughed at me laughing at them, and that's when it hit me: It's all a joke. With the possible exception of geometry, which has too many sharp edges, and health classes, which make you sick, it's all a joke. All of it. At least now. But I've only felt that way for a short time, so I might be wrong.

—Wil Neuton

WHEN he was finished with meditating and doing exercises the next morning, Wil took out the notebook and worked more on the piece about his grandmother. He could remember her so well, he thought, and yet when he tried to write about her and being with her, it would come out wrong. Not wrong, exactly, but just not complete. The words worked, but they didn't work right because he didn't know enough about how to use them. After an hour of writing, or trying to write about her, he put the pencil down and leaned back against the side of the boat.

The images that came to him were so clear, but when he tried to describe them—no, explain them . . . and there it was, there was the trouble with it. He wasn't writing about his grandmother. He was explaining her. And that, he thought, was not a way to learn about her, about what she had been to him.

He took up the notebook again and started to write, and this time he didn't explain or describe; he simply wrote what she meant to him, what she was as he saw her, and it thundered out of him. He could not stop it, and as he wrote he remembered more about her, small things, and he wondered, wondered that he could remember them now and have them be so real but not have known he was seeing them at the time.

Always there had been a loose hair that gave her trouble because it would hang down in her eyes, or her left eye. She would reach up with the back of her left wrist and push the hair away, push it back into the bun, and it would fall out and she would reach up and push it again. And the movement, the gesture, was as much a part of her as her name, or maybe even more than her name. Wil had seen it a thousand times, had forgotten it completely, didn't know that he'd known it, and when he found the picture in his mind now and wrote about it, he could remember each detail of each movement. The way her eye half closed, the way she blew a small puff of air out of the corner of her mouth as if to help by blowing the hair out of the way, the curve of her fingers, the thinness of her wrist and arm—all of it clear and open; it was something he never knew he was seeing until now.

He wrote it that way, writing all the things about her that he could think of, and when he was done he set the notebook aside again, put it in the pack, and took out his watercolors. He was thirsty, and he went to the spring for a drink, letting the cold water, so cold it almost hurt his teeth, slide down his throat. Then back to the boat-camp, where he opened the paints and tried to paint his grandmother and failed, as with the writing at first, failed and failed again because he could not make a person, could not make her look in the painting as he had actually seen her, known her.

But, he thought. *But it is me, not her, it is the painting, not the way she was that makes it difficult. It is the same as with the writing; the painting is the same because I am trying to paint the wrong thing. I am trying to paint—what? Paint a picture of her, and that is not what I want—I could use a camera if that is all I wanted. No. I do not want a picture of her; I want a picture that is her. The lines that made her, the colors that made her what she was—the same as with the writing—that is what I need to paint.*

He thought of how she pushed the hair away, the curve of her arm and the soft curve of the loose hair and the light gray of the color of her hair and the bright light on the bun at the back of her head, and he painted the lines, just the lines and the curves, and as with the writing it came then, came and roared out of him onto the paper in the soft colors of the water-based paints; out of him onto the paper, and he did one, then another—lines and colors mixed into thoughts that became his grandmother. And another and another into and through the afternoon, and it would not have stopped, could not have stopped except a voice came; a small voice came across the water.

"Wil. Wil—it's me, Susan."

He raised his head from the painting, stood and looked across the boat to the right. Past the end of the island he could see her standing on the shore waving, yelling. Her voice carried surprisingly well across the water.

"It's me," she repeated, cupping her hands to her mouth to yell. "Can I come out for a visit?"

So formal, he thought. *To ask that way.* He made an exaggerated nod so she could see it, waved, and put the paintings away. Then he carefully cleaned his brushes and put away the paint box and the notebook as well, all in the pack. It took him another minute or so to flip the boat over and push it out into the water, leaving the pack, and to get the oars in place and the boat turned.

With even strokes, sitting so he could see forward, he rowed around the end of the island and crossed the third of a mile or so to the shore where Susan waited. She was standing on an old poplar that had tipped and was hanging out over the water.

"I thought you'd be here." She jumped lightly from the tree down into the boat, taking her weight mostly on her hands. "I went by your house and saw your bike was gone . . . figured you'd be here."

"Did you talk to my folks?"

She shook her head—short jerks. "I could have, but when I saw your bike wasn't against the house I just turned around and came here. Funny way to row, sitting backward like that."

"It's so I can see where I'm going." Wil settled into the rhythm, pushing steadily for the island. "I missed some things when I rowed the other way. So."

She nodded but said nothing. She sat in the boat facing him, looking backward, and she studied him openly while he rowed. "The new Wil," she said at length.

"What?"

"I said it once before, but you've changed since I first met you. A lot."

"It's the island."

"The island? Oh, yes, you mentioned that before. What have you found there—some kind of treasure?"

He didn't answer. They were coming now around the end of the lagoon arm, and he eased off on the left oar and pulled with the right to turn the boat, then picked up speed to drive it up on the sand. Susan hopped out and helped him pull it up to the fire site, where he rolled it again and put the sticks under it to turn it into a lean-to. "My home," he said. "Quick and easy. I brought a tent but I didn't put it up when I found the boat worked so well."

"Didn't the mosquitoes tear you to pieces?"

"At first they were bad." Wil shrugged. "And I used repellent. But then I started a fire, and the smoke or smell kept them away. They didn't bother me at all."

She nodded skeptically, then turned from him. "So what do you do all the time out here?"

There is not a way, he thought, *to tell her. Not really a way.* "I sit, and think, or go swimming. Sometimes I write. Sometimes I paint."

She turned back. "Write and paint what?"

He smiled. "All sorts of things. Ants, my grandmother, water, sky. Would you like to see some of it?" *It's funny*, he thought, *but I don't feel shy anymore. Not even about showing her my work. She's right, I have changed.*

She came around the boat, and he reached into his pack and pulled out the notebook. As the paintings had dried he had put them in the back pages of the notebook, so they were all in one place, and he handed the whole package to Susan. She took it gently and sat against the boat and opened the pages, and he turned

back to the pack and dug around until he found the can of fruit cocktail. He opened it and held it and the spoon out to her, but she waved him away and kept looking at the notebook, so he drank the juice off—it was still cool from the shade of the pack—and ate about half the can. The sweetness tasted so rich it was almost too much, but it was delicious, and he had trouble stopping.

He pushed the lid back down on the can when he was done and put the uneaten portion back in the pack, making certain it did not tip. She was still reading, and he walked out on the flat rock and sat with his feet in the water. Initially his movement frightened the fish away, but he sat still, looking down into the water in the late afternoon, and they soon came back. Small sunfish and bluegills, four or five inches long, approached his feet warily, the courage of one drawing another until soon there were twenty or so. They seemed to hang in the water, absolutely still, and without moving a fin or seeming to they eased forward. Obviously they had to work to move, but he could not see the fins pushing. Still they slid through the water until two of them, two of the smaller ones, were close to his big toe. One of those two imperceptibly slid forward a tiny bit more and opened his mouth and tentatively took a nibble of the toe.

There were no teeth, and it tickled more than felt as a bite should feel, but the action of the first prompted the other small fish, which took a tiny nibble, and that brought the rest of them in, and soon they were all making nibbling passes on Wil's feet. He stood it as long as he could—when they nibbled on the bottom where he was ticklish it was so bad it almost made his back hurt to not move his feet—but at last his toes twitched.

In the smallest part of a second the fish vanished. All of them. With flashes of gold as they turned their sides they were gone, almost like an explosion. But he kept his feet still, and soon they were back, approaching cautiously at first, then bolder, then nibbling. And this time he gritted his teeth and kept from moving. In three or four minutes they realized that it was not food, and from that time on they did not come up to his feet. They did not swim away, but they did not approach, and he thought: *So, they can learn that fast; can learn a thing that fast and they are only fish. No, that isn't right either—they are not* only *fish. They are fish and they can learn a thing that fast and can remember a thing that well and they are fish. And people, only people, what can people do . . . ?*

Something touched the side of his head, the lightest of touches. And he turned to see Susan standing there, her hand out, with one finger touching his temple, and her eyes were soft and there were tears.

"What's wrong?" He stood up. "Are you all right?"

She shook her head. "Nothing is wrong. I just finished it—finished reading what you wrote about your grandmother and saw the paintings, and I don't know how to say it or what to say. It's almost as if it had been my grandmother and not just yours."

Wil didn't say anything for a moment, sat looking across the bay at the three loons. Then he smiled.

She sat next to him on the rock, feet in the water, using the back of her hand to dry her eyes. "Is that true? About your grandmother and all that? Is that all true?"

Again he said nothing. Then he nodded. "As true as

I can make it. And about the ants, too, and the heron and the loons and the sky—that's all true and that's what I'm doing on the island, trying to learn it, and that's why I'm going to stay on the island."

It slipped out. He hadn't even known that he was thinking it, hadn't known, and it slipped out.

"What do you mean?"

He looked at her. "I think I mean that I'm not leaving the island. At least not for a while. I'm going to stay out here and learn this . . . this thing that I'm here to learn. If I go back, if I don't stay and I go back, it will ruin it. Ruin it all."

"I'm not sure I understand . . ."

Wil sighed. "I'm not sure I do, either. But I know that if I leave here, if I go back without learning more, I will somehow lose what I am, and I don't want to do that. I don't ever want to do that."

"But how will you eat? You can't just live on bugs and things. How will you get food and stuff?"

He looked at her, said nothing, just looked.

"So all right," she said. "I can bring you food. And I will. But your parents—I mean, the whole world will think you've tipped over. They will think you're wacky. What about that?"

Again he looked, said nothing for a time, thinking. Then he shrugged. "I can't help the way they think or feel. My parents—my parents probably will have some trouble with it, and I don't want to hurt them. When you leave today, would you go by and tell them I'm all right?"

It was Susan's turn to stare. "You want me to be the one to tell your parents?"

"If I leave, if I leave to tell them even for that long,

116

they will work on me and I won't have this . . . this thing I have here. I may never get back. It will be gone, and I think if it goes it will be gone forever—what I've found on the island will just be gone. Dead.'' His voice was soft, but his eyes were tight at the corners, tight and sad. "I don't want it to go—not yet. Maybe not ever. You don't have to explain anything to them, or try to tell them what I'm doing. I'm not sure what I'm doing myself. Just tell them that I'm all right and that I'm going to stay on the island for a while. Will you do that?''

And after a time, after all of time, she nodded, because she had touched his temple and read about his grandmother and the heron and the loons and seen the paintings; she nodded and said she would help him, would help him, would help him. Then they sat for a time without speaking, until the sun was full of late-day heat, cooking them. And when it was so hot she was uncomfortable, she decided to go swimming before she had to bike home. She did not want to get her clothing wet, and so because she had touched him on the temple and read of his grandmother and would help him, would help him because they had understanding between them, she took off her clothes and swam in that manner. At first Wil did not look, but then of course he did, though not in that way, not in that way at all. It was more as he had looked at the heron or the sky, looking at her, and he took out the paint and painted her as she swam and sat to dry, painted her again and again until she dressed and came to sit alongside him near the boat.

By then it was close to the end of the daylight, so he rowed her back to shore, where she said she would bring food the next day. He waved at her as she biked down the road, and then turned back for the island. There was wood to gather for the night fire, and he wished to write of what had passed between them when she read about his grandmother and the heron and touched his temple. Somehow it was the same as his grandmother and the heron and the paintings of her sitting nude on the flat rock; somehow it was all the same, and he wished to write and write of it.

But nothing came right until that night and then what he wrote about was a frog.

FROG

By Wil Neuton

Once in biology, before we did fetal pigs, we had to
dissect frogs. We cut their little bellies open and all
looked at their little intestines and little stomachs and
little hearts and little eyes and little brains and when
we did this we were supposed to learn two things—
we were supposed to learn and know all about frogs,
and we were supposed to learn and be amazed at the
"miracle of life."

Well.

I thought that maybe we did learn a lot. I could
identify all the parts of a frog's guts and could draw a
picture of a frog's guts when I got done. The picture
is good, with arrows pointing to all the different parts
I found with my scalpel and tiny wooden stick used
for poking.

But later, on the island, I saw a heron suddenly
snake its head down and grab a frog—not spear but
grab; they don't spear with their beaks—and flip it
around in the air twice to get it positioned right and
swallow it down, alive, straightening its throat to
take the still live, still kicking frog down into its
stomach. And I thought then that from biology I
learned almost absolutely nothing about frogs except
how their guts looked and that is next to nothing.

If you wanted to learn about something, is that a

way to do it? Say you wanted to know another person—would you dip him in alcohol, kill him, flip him up on a table and push his guts around with a stick to know him?

That's what happened to my thinking and so I set out to learn about a frog and watch a frog because I already knew how one frog's day ended, how he ended in the heron's stomach.

I found a frog in the shallows on the edge of the bay and I crawled as far as I could to get close without scaring him and I watched him all afternoon, and maybe I don't still know all about frogs but I know more than I did when I just poked around in their guts.

He—I thought of him as a he—was a big green frog, with black spots, the kind I think are called leopard frogs, and when I first saw him he was sitting on the edge of an old piece of wood. He sat there for over an hour and it was hard to just watch because he did nothing for that time. But finally a bug landed on the wood next to him and he leaned slightly to the right, without moving his feet, and his tongue shot out and the sticky end hit the bug and pulled it back into the frog's mouth, where he swallowed it, still alive, gulping three or four times to get the wiggling feet and flapping wings down.

Then he went back to sitting. After another half hour or so he slid off the piece of wood into the water, dove to the bottom and lay there where I could see him next to a small weed—a minute or so—then came back up and climbed onto the log again. I guessed that the sun was drying his skin and he had to moisten it.

Then nothing again, just sitting, and of course I was getting bored with it and was just about to give it up, figuring maybe I had gone too far this time and expected a bit much of a single frog, or maybe had a boring frog, when he suddenly tensed.

I could see nothing, but he tensed all up and froze and in a few seconds I could see a water snake come by. It was small, a small brown snake—not much bigger than the frog—and it had been in the weeds near the bank and went about a foot away from the frog and I thought he would jump in the water but instead he sat, still, and watched it swim by. The only movement was a trembling in the muscles of his back legs, to be ready, and his eyeballs rotating to watch the snake and I could see that he was afraid.

And what a thing, I thought, for a frog to be afraid. When you're poking around in their guts you somehow don't think of them being afraid, or being able to have fear.

But he did. He had fear. When the snake had passed and was well gone down the bank the frog relaxed, settled back down on the piece of wood, and spent another half hour before he dived into the water to moisten his skin again, then crawl up on the log, and so his day went until, in the early evening, he suddenly swelled up his throat and began to sing.

It wasn't a croak so much as a high-pitched trilling sound, a song. He did it again and again, his body extended, singing from his log, his place, and perhaps it was to find a mate but that isn't what he got. Instead, after he had sung eight or ten times, another frog came toward the log, swimming with even strokes and again the frog on the log tensed. The new frog tried to push him off but he grabbed and they wrestled for control of the piece of wood, pushing and fighting, with great heaves of their legs until the original frog succeeded in pushing the new frog away, two, three times and he swam away.

Then he sang again and this time the song was a small bit different, perhaps a bit lower and louder. He had felt anger and had fought and had felt fear of the snake and had defended his territory and I thought two things, two things from the time with the frog. I thought: Where does that show, where does the fear and anger and pride and song show when you are poking in the frog's gut with a stick and where, I thought, is the frog different from me?

14

I sometimes have difficulty with time. I was doing all right until one day I thought of it. Just thought of it. I was sitting there in study period with everything going kind of blank the way it does in study period, and I thought of time. Which is silly. Time is nothing. But I thought of time and how it is different for everybody and how you can make it go slow or fast by either going to a dentist or a good movie, and I was really getting into it, really cooking on time, when Mr. Musovich, who teaches social studies and had the study hall, pinned me with his eyes and said, ''Neuton, quit dreaming and wasting your time.'' And I started to tell him that I was just thinking about time and how I wasn't sure I could waste it because there wasn't really anything to it to waste and how I wasn't really sure it was my time to waste or not waste because how could anybody own time or have his own time, but Mr. Musovich is also the football coach and has a large neck and shoulders, and so I didn't say anything. But I still sometimes have difficulty with time.

—Wil Neuton

AFTER dark he wrote more of what had happened that day and tried to make it right and then tried to paint. But the light from the fire was not good enough, and after one attempt at a form cutting through water, swimming in water with the light around it, he decided to wait until day and put the paper and brushes away and went back to writing. He sat that way, working with the pen, trying to make the words act as perhaps paint should act because he really wanted to paint what he was trying to write. He finally put it all away.

He found some canned spaghetti and meatballs in the pack and opened them and heated them by the edge of the fire. When they were warm on one side he ate them slowly, chewing carefully. He was hungry now, fiercely hungry, and the taste of the food made it worse. When he was done with the can, he wished he had another, and still another, but instead he went to the spring in the dark—ducking and brushing mosquitoes as soon as he was away from the protection of the fire—and drank water. He had read somewhere or had been told by a teacher, he couldn't remember which, that it was better to stay a little hungry when you were painting or writing, working in the arts. He still didn't think of himself as an artist so much as somebody who was trying to learn. But it was also probably true, he thought, that you could think better if you were hungry, and he had to think, wanted to think better. So he drank water to fill his stomach, and it eased the hunger.

One night, he thought. *I have really only been here one night.*

Back at the fire he stretched out on his bag under the boat and pulled the loose fold over the top and put his head down. Sleep did not come at once, but slowly, as a friend might come to help him rest, and when it did come he fell asleep watching the red coals from the fire die, his face hot with the day's sun on the water off the bay and heat from the coals. The last thing he heard was the night cry of the loon across the water, and an answer from the other side, both sounds sliding across the still lake like mercury.

Then sleep.

He was awakened by a storm of bird songs. They sang high and trilling notes; dozens, hundreds of them had hit the island trees on their way across the lake, and he opened his eyes to find two of them sitting on the edge of the fire inspecting the coals. They were waxwings, silver gray with crested tops, and they cocked their heads sideways; and when he turned to get out from under the boat they flew, taking the flocks with them, leaving him in silence. Like an alarm shut off in mid-ring.

This time he knew exactly where he was, knew exactly about the boat over him and the burned-out fire and the morning sun. He had slept on one shoulder all night and was stiff. When he was on his feet, he stretched and took off his clothes and ran into the lake. The water was only mildly cool, holding day-heat from the day before, and he did a small lap of the bay in a slow crawl and wished he had a snorkel and mask to see what he was swimming over. In his mind he made a mental list: more pens and pencils, better brushes and paints, more paper, better paper, a mask and snorkel, a cap—things he would like if he had a way to get them without leaving the island. Maybe Susan?

On the beach he used the edge of his hand to wipe the water off, then walked to the flat rock and did his meditation exercises. It was still hard to open his mind, although slightly easier than before, and when he finally triggered the blankness he found his parents there, in his thoughts. They would come soon, he knew, and they wouldn't understand and he wouldn't be able to make them understand, but that was not what he thought about. They could come soon and want him to return to the house with them, but that's not what he thought about either.

Instead he remembered a time from when he was a small boy of maybe four or five and his father had bought him his first bike. He could remember the bike exactly. A small bike, a dirt bike with knobby wheels and a gear shift on the right handlebar—three forward speeds and a pedal brake and all over a shining silver. His father had been smiling, and Wil could not ride, had never ridden a two-wheeler, and somehow his father had not thought of that, had never thought of it. He'd just assumed that when he brought the bike home Wil would be able to jump on it and start riding it.

Of course Wil tried. He straddled it, but even though it was small he couldn't reach the ground on both sides of the bar with his feet. He was that young yet. So he fell. And fell again and again, every time he tried to get on the bike, until his father held the bike up, held it while he got on and put his feet on the pedals.

Wil had that now in his mind: His father helping him to learn to ride the two-wheeler and his mother watching and what finally happened when he learned to ride. He knew he would write all of that the way he wrote of his grandmother.

In time, in the morning sun, with a gentle morning breeze lapping the water against the rock, he finished his movements, the almost-dance movements that had been the meditation and the thoughts of learning to ride the bike. He went back to the fire and took his pants and T-shirt from the boat where he'd laid them and got dressed. The morning sun had warmed them and taken the night dampness out of them, from sleeping in them.

He was hungry, and he dug through his diminishing stock in the pack and found the partial can of fruit cocktail, still cool from the night. This he ate slowly, staring across the bay with his eyes glazed, thinking of nothing, thinking of everything. The loons were out there, diving and swimming and moving with each other, and he thought of painting them. But they were hard to see to paint, were just low and black on the water, sometimes with only their heads showing. When Susan swam, they had been afraid because they did not know her, and they had moved out of the bay, not flying but swimming, and he thought then, sitting with the almost empty can of fruit cocktail, that they knew so much. Even the loons knew so much. They could tell different people, had the knowledge of people being not the same, and he couldn't look at two adult loons and tell the difference. Even though they were different. *Those three out there in the bay are all different*, he thought, watching them swim, *but I can only tell that because the two young ones are not the same size. When they're grown I will not know the loons.*

Perhaps when I am grown I will not know anything. Perhaps that is the way it works, the way it is with growing. When you grow, you start to unlearn things.

It was then he heard the motor. It came from across the lake, by the road and in back of the island. The sound was faint, a sputtering start, a stop, then another

127

start, and it caught and held in a whine that came not only above the water but through the lake as well, through the water. A cutting sound.

He waited, thought for a moment it might be fishermen but knew, really, who it was, who it had to be. In five minutes the boat came around the left end of the island and turned into the bay. It was a small aluminum boat, a fourteen-footer, and his parents were in it. His father sat in the stern, steering, and his mother sat up in the bow. She waved when she saw Wil, and he answered the wave and stood to walk down to the beach and pull the boat up on the sand. She was wearing a pair of jeans and a sweatshirt and a cap that said a name of a beer across the front, though she didn't drink. His father was in a windbreaker and was wearing a cap that said BERRYMAN across the front surrounded by lightning bolts.

"What a charming place." Wil's mother jumped out of the boat. "This little harbor and little beach. Just beautiful. Like a little Bermuda that nobody knows about. I see why you like it." But her voice was a little too controlled, too tight.

His dad clambered across the seats, jumped out, then turned back and brought a cooler out. "We brought some goodies from the store. Pop and lunchmeat and a couple of sandwiches and chips. You know. Junk food."

He finished the sentence and there was silence, and the silence grew until it went too far, too long, and became embarrassing. Wil's father coughed and his mother poked a hair back up under her cap, and Wil thought how much like his grandmother's action his mother's movements were.

128

"I guess Susan came by the house last night," Wil said, finally. "I asked her to tell you . . ."

"Tell us what?" His father had been bending down to the cooler and now stood, an edge to his voice. "That you had decided to live on an island and worry your mother half sick . . ."

"I'm not half sick."

". . . and then not tell us yourself. Actually send a girl we don't even know to tell us? Is that what you were going to tell us? Like that?"

Another silence. Wil looked across the bay. The loons were gone, gone from the motor sound of the boat. Gone in fear. "I started to explain it to you the other night, when I came, but to be honest I don't understand it completely myself. It's just that, that I am learning something out here about myself, about life, about everything, and if I leave I will lose it. . . ."

"I just want to know if it's drugs." His father held up a hand. "Is it drugs?"

La, la, Wil thought. *Somehow I should have known that was coming, and I didn't even think of it.* "No. No drugs. It's more than that, more than drugs could ever be. It's that I'm learning. Learning all the time somehow. By staying alone out here. I've been painting and writing and studying and meditating . . ."

"Meditating?"

"Yes. I sit or stand and do movements and meditate, and it makes my mind blank and clear thoughts come in. . . ." He trailed off as he realized they were both staring at him. His mother's mouth was actually open a bit. A fly had landed on her cheek, and she didn't raise a hand to brush it off. His father had a can of pop in one hand and the other frozen on the fliptop. "I mean I realize it sounds kind of crazy . . ."

After a time his father sighed. "It almost sounds like you've gotten involved in some kind of religious cult. But how could that have happened? And how long are you going to stay out here? A week, a month? How long?"

"I don't know. As long as it takes," Wil said, shrugging. And then repeated himself. "The time it takes . . ." But his father wasn't listening and had not asked the question expecting to be answered.

"I mean, meditating," he went on, "and doing movements and going crazy like this—it sounds just like a cult. How did you get involved with a cult? Was it back in Madison before we moved? Or did that girl—sure, that's it, isn't it? It's the girl . . ."

"Dad. Dad, stop now. No, it isn't the girl. She just said she'd come by and tell you for me. I was afraid if I came by you'd make me stay home. And it isn't a cult. It's never been a cult."

"What did we do?" His mother cut in. She had been standing still, her mouth slightly open. She brushed the fly away. "I always thought things were going all right. I understand that you might not like the move north from Madison . . ."

"What do you mean, not like the move?" his father interrupted. "We had to do it. It was a chance to move up and get out of the city. . . ."

And they started bickering, which they had never done. They had argued perhaps, but not this way, with tiny voices cutting at each other; and Wil stood and watched them, and the feeling came that in many ways it was almost a play, with people saying what they were supposed to say and do. And he thought then that in many ways all of living was a play, or could be a play, or should be a play as all of life could or should be a painting or could or should be written. So it could be learned. And he loved them then, loved them with a depth he had never thought he could feel, loved them but could not understand how it was that they could not understand him. Or try to understand him. They had always seemed to be good about it, but there was something this time they couldn't get past, some part of what he was doing they couldn't see, and he knew only that he had to do it. More than anything in his life he had to do this.

So they bickered until it ran out, and they turned to see him standing there. His mother said nothing, but his father shook his head and said that he didn't know, didn't know what had happened but that it was very strange and that he was worried about Wil but he wouldn't force him to leave the island—yet. He said it that way . . . yet. With a delay on it. Because he wasn't sure that would help Wil, to make him leave, help him with whatever his problem was, whatever it turned out to be. Something psychological, he said—it was something psychological, the problem. And he was worried about Wil, he said again, and would try to find help for him, and they would go now because they weren't sure what else to do.

Then they got in the boat, and there was strain between them, a change between them that Wil didn't think had to be there now but was. He pushed them out, and his father fired up the motor, and they were soon out of sight.

When they were gone, Wil stood a moment, looking

across the bay, wondering if there were really something "psychological" about him, a problem he could not know about because if he knew, it wouldn't be a problem—one of those weird things. But as he stood, the loons came back around the left point and into the bay; then when the motor sound was completely gone the bird sounds came back, and he decided it didn't matter. He was not what he had been before, and his parents were not what they had been, and a great sadness was there, was part of that knowledge, but still it was so. He was what he was, and if he was wrong or had mental problems, that was still the way he was, the way he had to live.

He was what the island had made him and continued to make him. And there was work to do, more work this day than he thought he would ever be able to do in his life. He had to try and understand what had happened, how the play worked.

BICKERBITS

An aid play to help understand and deal with adults

By Wil Neuton

CHARACTERS: *A mother, a father, and a young person.*

SETTING: *A typical home in a typical neighborhood. The parents are standing in a typical kitchen, the father next to a typical refrigerator, holding a typical pickle from which he is about to take a typical bite. The mother is near the typical coffee machine, where she has just poured a cup of typical coffee and is about to take a typical sip when the child walks in and puts one hand on the typical refrigerator door to reach in and get something to eat. The father stops with the pickle a foot from his mouth; the mother holds the cup just in front of her lips. The steam comes up to her nose.*

CHILD: "Hi, Mom. Hi, Dad. Any leftover chicken?"

Already the child has made several basic mistakes, all critical. Never bomb in and greet adults when they are having a conversation. Their attention rapidly refocuses from the conversation to the interruption—in this case the child with his hand on the refrigerator door. Also, never ask if there is food. This is a sore point with adults, who always think young people eat too much, snack too much, and accuse them regularly of ruining

*their appetites, which makes no sense because if they
ruined their appetites they wouldn't be hungry all the
time—but there you are. It is also important to not in-
terrupt an adult who is about to take a sip of coffee, as
this puts a blip in their ritual, and a ritual blip
changes any adult's whole train of thought. And never,
never under any circumstances should a child cut into a
conversation where the father is holding either a pickle
or carrot or piece of celery—these vegetables too easily
become pointers. In this case the young person is dead
meat on several counts, but he is too involved in the
food to sense danger.*

FATHER: "Hello, son [or daughter]." (*The father low-
ers the pickle.*) "Are you sure you want to eat left-
overs between meals?"

*A silly question. The young person is starving, and
what he really wants to do is unhinge his lower jaw
and tip the contents of the refrigerator into his mouth.
But it isn't a question anyway. The father is merely
opening up the conversation, getting ready to Help
Straighten Out the young person's life. The mother low-
ers the cup.*

MOTHER: "You know, you've been worried about
your complexion. All this snacking doesn't help it."

FATHER: "Just this morning I found three candy
wrappers in your room. . . ." (*Up comes the pickle,
points first at the ceiling, then at the young person.*)
"And that's another thing I've wanted to speak to
you about. Your room looked upside-down this

morning, and what was that dead thing under the bed with the tail sticking out?"

CHILD: "I . . ."

MOTHER: "A disorganized mind can lead to severe mental problems as you get older. It may seem like just a messy room now, but when you're an adult you might find yourself becoming confused. Do you want to be confused?"

CHILD: "I . . ."

FATHER: (*The pickle waves now, pointing up and then down at the young person.*) "Speaking of confusion, how can you help it, listening to that music so loud? And how can you listen to anybody called The Ruptured Spleen in the first place?"

CHILD: "I . . ."

MOTHER: "Oh, I don't know about that. I like some of the music. I don't think that's as confusing as a disorganized existence, do you?"

FATHER: "Disorganized isn't the word for it. And I'd settle for him having a confused existence if I could get him to clean his room and carry out the garbage and edge the driveway and sidewalk and straighten out the garage."

CHILD: "I . . ."

MOTHER: "I think you're coming down a bit hard on him, don't you? All of those things at once might make him even more confused."

FATHER: (*The pickle swings like a gun and aims at the mother.*) "When I was his age, I used to have to walk six miles barefoot through broken glass carrying an anvil on my back just to get a chance to work geometry with a broken pencil. . . ."

Or something like that. There's always some hard thing they had to do, but it really doesn't matter. At this point they start bickering, the problem moves away from the young person, and he (or she) can quietly get the piece of chicken and go to his (or her) room to see what crawled under his (or her) bed and died. But the main thing is to understand the bickering.
What causes it is not known for sure. It could be chicken, or putting a hand on a refrigerator door, eating, weather, coffee, or pickles—research isn't complete yet.
What is known is that it always centers around young people but is rarely aimed at them, and it always ends the same way.

FATHER: "Well, I just thought . . ."

MOTHER: "Well, I don't know if it's all that important."

The father bites the pickle, and the mother takes a sip of coffee, and they start talking about Something Important, the young person completely forgotten.

15.

When I was in the seventh grade, I had a short time when I was caught up in competition. I wanted to be good at something—not just good, I wanted to be better than other people at it. I didn't ride bikes much then, but I had long legs, so I decided to compete at running. Every day I ran. Every day. Ran to school, ran home, ran to movies, ran to the store. And as I ran, I got really strong. I actually got faster than some of the other runners on the seventh-grade track team. But no matter what I did, there were some I couldn't get as fast as; no matter how much I ran, there were some I couldn't beat. So there I was, stuck in the middle. Running and running and stuck in the middle. Then one day Petey Welms stopped me and said, "How come you're running all the time? What are you scared of? Every time I want to talk to you, you're running. The other day I called to get you over because we had seven new movies to watch—all fright flicks—and your mother said you were out running. Running? Why?" And of course I couldn't answer him. I could have told him that I wanted to run so I could get faster than some people but not as fast as some other people, but Petey wouldn't have followed the logic in that. And neither did I. And that's when I quit being competitive. It just doesn't work for me.

—Wil Neuton

SUDDENLY, suddenly the bay changed. Wil was standing on the rock, doing once again the movements of the heron. It was about noon, the sun almost directly overhead, and he had taken his shirt off to feel the heat but kept his jeans on because the backs of his knees were burned and sore and he wanted them covered. The movements were not right, lacked the grace of the heron, the still, frozen grace, and he thought that if he could torque his arms more, pushing until there was pain to make more of a curve, it would be right. And the bay changed.

Changed. For a second, a moment, there was a new stillness, almost a stopping somehow, and then the loons rose in frantic flight, slamming along the water until they were airborne, the mother first, then the two young ones lifting, skipping off the water, and they were gone.

He swiveled his head to look, studied the sky, the island, all around, and could see nothing, hear nothing—but he could sense it, could smell-feel it somehow. It filled all of him. Something dangerous had happened to the bay, some strange new threat he didn't understand, and he sat on the rock and stared at the water and felt the hair go up on the back of his neck and could not tell why.

He thought then that it was something from his parents, something left from them, and it had somehow come through him and into the bay, but that didn't work either because they didn't threaten him and most certainly did not threaten the loons, threaten the bay . . . then he saw it.

Directly in front of him, not thirty feet away in the

stillness of the water a sudden dark point appeared. It was the shape of an arrowhead, pointed, with two small holes in the end, and it hissed a tiny hiss of air, hung for a moment, then without a ripple sank back beneath the surface of the water. Wil could see the dark line of an ancient shell; a shell as old as time, a gray-black ridged shell the color of rotten mud broke the surface and rolled under and moved toward Wil and the rock.

Snapping turtle. It was huge, easily sixty or seventy pounds, with a head as big as Wil's fist. And it came as if drawn to him. Wil pulled his feet away from the water and slowly stretched out on the rock so he would be low and present no silhouette to frighten the turtle because he wanted to see it. He had seen them before, sometimes crossing the road in the spring, while biking outside of Madison. They moved a lot in spring, he learned from a biology teacher, looking for a good place to lay their eggs. But he'd never seen one in the water, swimming, hunting—whatever it was doing.

With his face at the edge of the rock he propped his chin on his hand and became still, watched.

There was virtually no wind, and the water in the bay was settled and clear. He could see the dark shape, somehow ominous, sliding along the bottom, and there was still the feeling of fear, of quietness in the water. Once he had read in a sporting magazine about a diver off the coast of Australia who had been hit and nearly torn in half by a great white shark. The man had been fishing, spearing, and he'd said that just before the shark hit him the ocean had suddenly gone very quiet—a stillness as the shark moved on him.

That same feeling was in the water of the bay now as the turtle came toward the rock. The loons were long gone, the fish were gone—even the small sunfish by the rock—and it was all because of the turtle, the dark shape sliding along the bottom.

Now it rose again, at an angle toward Wil's face and right in front of him; four feet away now, it broke the surface with its pointed nose and again took air in a small hiss. Then it settled toward the bottom, not swimming but sinking. When it was near the base of the rock, it turned, facing out, and backed in under a small overhang. There it stopped moving, lay still.

Wil had to inch his face slightly forward to see the front of the turtle, there beneath him, still and waiting. For a moment Wil thought the turtle was just resting. It sat so still, so silent. But there wasn't much sense in resting the way it was, backed under the overhang, and the more he studied the turtle down there the more he felt as if the turtle were doing more than resting. He was waiting.

He was hunting. He was waiting for something to kill, something to kill and eat.

And now Wil remembered the sunfish—how when he first put his feet in they all swam away in fear, afraid of the movement. But then, as he had kept still, they all came back, they'd come back and moved in on his feet and gotten closer and closer. . . .

Even as he thought of them, he saw the small ones swimming back into the shadow of the rock. And again, at first they were wary, were cautious of the large gray shape tucked into the overhang, but the fear didn't last.

They got closer and closer, as they had with Wil's feet and legs, and he thought now that perhaps he should warn them, should make a motion, but that would be wrong, too. The turtle was part of it, as with the heron and the frog and the loons and the small fish the loons ate. So Wil lay and watched, watched as the small sunfish grew bolder and bolder, and he saw the one, the one that was marked for it, saw that fish as it worked around some weed and came closer and closer to its death.

When it came it was stunning, so violent and rapid that it made Wil jump. The fish moved forward, away from the weed, and seemed to hover with no effort not more than two inches in front of the turtle's beak. Still it was not close enough. Still the turtle waited. Then the sunfish moved the last part, the last part of its life, moved perhaps a quarter of an inch closer to the turtle, and the head slammed forward out of the shell, the gaping jaws took the fish in the middle, in the soft part of the belly. The water was full of blood and guts and a froth of scales, was full of the debris of the end of the sunfish's life, and the fish was stiff and curved in the rigor of death around the head of the turtle, and it was done.

Done.

I have seen the end now, Wil thought. *I have seen the end of a thing here.* The turtle made certain the fish was positioned right and swallowed it, still twitching, but it was over before that for Wil. It was over when the fish was still two inches from the turtle and safe and moved that next tiny part of an inch and was dead. That's when it was done. Not when the turtle hit the fish, not when the turtle swallowed the sunfish, but when the fish was two inches away and moved the last part of its life into the curve of death. That's when it ended for the fish. *Perhaps*, Wil thought, *that's when it ends for all of us, not when it ends but when it's still going, getting ready to end.*

The turtle was done. He came up for air once again, and this time Wil must have moved his eyes, or blinked, because the turtle saw him and dove away with speed, heading out of the bay. Wil sat up to watch him go, then stood, but lost the shape forty feet away, still heading out into the lake.

He was standing that way, still thinking of the end of the sunfish, when he heard the cry from the bank and looked over to see Susan standing on the shore waving. She was holding up a duffel bag with one hand, and it looked full of supplies. Wil went to the boat and turned it over and headed for shore.

16.

Not everybody makes the same kind of mistake. At least that's what I've found. If, say, an adult is walking down the sidewalk and drops a sack of groceries, it's just that: somebody dropped a sack of groceries. But if a kid is bringing home groceries and drops them, it's a natural disaster, like it's the last sack of groceries in the world and everybody in Yugoslavia is going to starve because the kid dropped the groceries. It's the same mistake, only different. I decided when I was seven that I would only make the adult kinds of mistakes. But that's one of those things that sounds good and isn't. It hasn't worked out. Oh, I made adult mistakes all right. Still do. But I get blamed for them as a kid.

—Wil Neuton

SUSAN jumped out of the boat first and helped pull it up on the sand. Then she took out the duffel bag and kneeled next to it, opening the top snap. "Packages for the needy."

Wil flipped the boat and propped it and sat next to her in the sand. "You don't have to bring stuff all the time. . . ."

"That is something you don't have to say."

"Right. I know that. It just slipped out. It's all the beatings my dad gave me when I was young to make me polite. I should know better than that."

"I just meant that between us, you know, you don't have to say things like that—just polite things. I think what you're doing here is great, and if I can help a little I'd like to be able to do it. It's almost like a natural feeling."

"Can I thank you?"

She studied him. "Yes."

"Thank you."

"You're welcome."

"So."

"So look at all the loot." She dug in the bag. "I found some more paints for you—an old watercolor set I had but never used. And it has some brushes in a little case. And another notebook. And an old box of wooden pencils . . ."

Wil took the pencils and watercolors as she held them out, placed them gently on the sand in front of him, lined them up carefully. The watercolor box was a metal one, similar to his except larger. He opened it, and the colors were rich. There were twice as many of them as well, and the brushes were in a small side case; when he opened it, he could tell they were of quality. Some were thick, some thinner, and there were two small fine-point brushes for detail work. The pencils were in an old wooden case that had a picture of a jumping deer on the lid. He opened it to see a dozen reddish cedar pencils, natural-wood-colored, with red erasers. Nestled in the box with them was a small metal sharpener, the kind you hold in your fingers and twist around to shave the wood. "They're beautiful—so old and fine."

She smiled. "One of my aunts gave me the colors and pencils when I was small. I just never got into drawing or painting. I like writing, but mostly I like movement."

"Like dance."

"Sort of—yes. Maybe dance. But work, too. I like to work. To get tired with it and feel pushed to where it's hard to do. That kind of thing. I've never tried dance, you know, like you see it on television sometimes."

"Neither did I until now. Well, maybe not now. I don't know if it's dance or just trying to understand things. I've been doing exercises, then thinking about birds and waves and wind and things when I do them and trying to become them, and maybe that's the same as dance." He held up the pencils. "But these are special. Maybe you shouldn't give them to me."

"That's exactly why I want you to have them." She looked at him again, eyes open, straight into his. "What you're doing here is special, maybe more special than you think. The other night I told my mom and dad about it and my brother, and we talked about it all night."

"What did they think?"

"Dad and my brother at first thought you might be crazy, but after a while Dad decided you were somebody who had the light on him—that's how he put it—somebody who had the light on him and needs to be encouraged. My brother still thinks you're crazy. . . ."

"Maybe I am. My folks came out this morning, and they're pretty sure I'm cracked. At least that's the way they acted." He took a few minutes and told Susan about the visit with his parents, how they wound up arguing and they never argued, and how they left with everything up in the air. "So I don't know. Maybe they're right. Maybe your brother is right."

Susan looked across the bay for a moment, then shook her head. "The way things are, there's not a way to tell if somebody is crazy or not. Not the way things are. But my mom—I didn't tell you what my mom said. She never did agree that you were crazy or had the light on you. She was sitting at the kitchen table, and she looked at my dad and said you were gifted, that you were one of the thirsty people who needed to know things and we should help you. That's what she said. And she even baked you an apple pie to back it up— if I didn't bust it pedaling from my place to here. You ever tried riding a bike while carrying a dufflebag with an apple pie inside?"

No, Wil thought, *I never have*. But he didn't say anything. He was thinking how he had sat in her kitchen; he had sat in her kitchen, and this lady knew him that well, and he couldn't remember how she looked. Susan brought out cans of food and a sweatshirt—"I borrowed it from my brother for when the nights get cold"— and finally the pie, only slightly dented and looking wonderful wrapped in clear plastic. And through it all he could think of nothing except that he didn't even remember how Susan's mother looked. When the supplies were all stacked under the boat, they went out on the rock and sat next to each other and let the late afternoon sun cook them.

After a moment he cleared his throat. "Tell me about your mother."

"What?"

"Your mother. Tell me about her. I don't know anything about her, and here this woman sends me a pie and says I should be helped, and I can't even remember how she looks. Would you tell me about her?"

"Really?"

He nodded. "Really."

"Well . . . I don't know where to start."

"Start with her age, how she looks, what she thinks, everything you can. What she eats. All of it. I want to know about her. . . ."

"The thirst—she said you were one of the thirsty ones."

He smiled. "I guess so. . . . Tell me about her."

So Susan sat in the sun on the rock and told Wil as much as she could about her mother, as much as she knew, and he sat with his eyes closed and listened and tried to learn about her. After an hour of solid talk she was still only up to when her mother went to high school—was amazed at how much she knew about her mother—and leaned back on her elbow to get more comfortable to continue, when Wil held up his hand. "Hold it."

"What's the matter?"

"I don't know. I heard something. . . ." He listened for a few seconds with his breath held. "Something . . . there. There it is. It's a motor. An outboard starting up."

Susan nodded. "I hear it now. It's over in back. Maybe it's your folks coming out again."

"Maybe, but I don't think so. He said they wouldn't. No, it's somebody else." He stood away from her, listened to the motor for another moment, then trotted back across the beach and into the trees to the other side of the island. He didn't step out of the tree line but stayed hidden and didn't know why but was glad. Coming across the lake were three boys in a small aluminum boat with an outboard, and back at the shore was an old pickup parked where he had his bike hidden.

Ray Bunner was sitting at the motor, steering the boat.

Oh good, Wil thought. *This is good. Maybe this is just my day to get problems out of the way. La, la.*

He turned and trotted back to the beach and found Susan standing by the boat. "It's Ray Bunner and two others."

"Rats! I hoped they wouldn't come. . . ."

"I wonder how they knew where I was—I mean, so fast?"

She stared at him. "I forgot you were from the city. Welcome to the country. News travels fast in the country. Everybody knows you're out here, everybody. You're the talk of the countryside. You'd be amazed at how soon people knew it. In fact there might have been some who knew it before you came out to the island."

The motor was getting loud now as the boat came to the end of the island and started around. Wil shrugged. "Well, there's nothing to do but talk to him."

"Talk to him?" She stared. "Didn't I tell you at the cafe you'd probably have to fight him?"

"Well, we'll see. Usually you can talk these things out. I remember one time I was having some trouble in Madison with a guy who spent a lot of time crushing pop cans. He did it with his fingers and decided he didn't like me. But we talked it over for a while and . . ."

"Ray Bunner doesn't talk. I'm not sure he even knows how to talk, unless you count single-syllable grunts. Forget the talking. You'd better be ready to get physical. Maybe I could help. You get him listening to you, and

I'll drop the boat on him. It won't stop him, but it might slow him down until we can call in an air strike . . ."

She trailed off as the boat came around the end of the island and into the bay, the three boys sitting, leaning forward, waiting to hit the beach, Wil thought, like Marines assaulting an enemy island. Wil stood away from Susan, moved down to the beach and stood on the sand, waiting.

None of it took long. Ray ran the boat up onto the sand, let the motor drive it up until it stopped, and then stepped out without getting his feet wet. The two boys with him jumped out and stood in back of him. Ray walked up to Wil, squared his shoulders, turned sideways and spit, barely missing Wil's bare foot. *I wonder,* Wil thought, *what I would have done if he had spit on my foot. Wash it off in the lake, I guess.*

"Shoot," Ray said. "You ain't much, are you?"

See, Wil thought silently to Susan, *you were wrong. He can so talk. He got out a whole sentence.* "I guess not. I ain't never been much. . . ." *Might as well agree with him.*

"I told you guys," Ray said, speaking over his shoulder to the two boys who were with him. "Shoot, I said, he ain't much to have everybody talking about him like that. Just another city turd up here showing off, taking our women . . ."

Two sentences, Wil thought. *No, almost three. Too many.* "Taking your women?"

Ray nodded toward Susan. "Her. Dragging her out here against her will, probably. Stealing our women. . . ."

Susan stepped forward. "Dammit, Ray Bunner, you watch your filthy mouth or I'll tell my big brother, and he'll tune you right up, you hear? There isn't anything like that going on here. Your problem is you just couldn't stand the attention he was getting. You want everybody to be talking about you, what you're doing or what you were doing or what you are going to do. You just can't stand it that somebody else gets some attention. That's your problem.'' She put her hands on her hips, her voice snapping like a whip. ''The real reason you came out here in the boat is to beat up on Wil. That's all you're here for, so let's get it out of the way so you can leave.''

Now wait a minute, Wil thought. *This isn't quite how I had it all planned. I meant we would talk it out, you know.* He held up his finger. ''Now just a minute, Ray. That isn't quite how I would—''

Which is as far as he got. When he raised his hand, Ray took it for a hostile action; he brought his right hand up from his waist, put a lot of shoulder in it, and caught Wil on the side of the head with a sound like a board hitting a melon. Wil wasn't prepared for it, didn't see it coming, and, when he thought of it later, realized that it wouldn't have made any difference if he had seen it coming.

He went down on one knee. He knew that much. He heard Susan scream something, and he went down on one knee with the blow, felt blood come to his ear and the side of his cheek from the split on the cheekbone. He knew that much. Down on one knee and the taste of blood coming into the side of his mouth from the split cheek, and he knew that much. And if it had stopped there—

If it had ended there, nothing would have come of it. Had it ended there, Wil would not have done what he did.

Wil was still controlling himself. He shook his head a little, felt sharp jabs of pain with the shake, but still controlled. He started to stand, started to say that it was done, all done, and Ray hit him again. This time a short blow with his left that came straight and hard and caught Wil on the forehead and knocked him back and down, back and down on the sand.

Rolling colors, splashing and flashing with the pain from the blow, tearing his mind open . . . He came up on an elbow, tried to see, couldn't, then could and saw a pain-dream of Susan—Susan coming over him to fly at Ray, screaming, "Sucker-punch, sucker-punch"— and still controlling, still holding it, but then he saw or thought he saw Ray's hand come out to slap or seem to slap Susan down, and Wil changed.

Later he would try to make the change happen in his mind to learn from it, to write of it or paint it, but he could not.

When he saw Ray's hand come out to push or slap Susan, there was almost an audible click in his brain, a sudden shift, and he was under water, under the overhanging rock, and he wasn't Wil, wasn't Wil trying to learn or know or feel. He saw only the blue water and knew coldness, certainty. The fish, he thought, the fish has come the last quarter of an inch, and he had only now to strike, to see the spray of blood and scales in the water, hit with all that he was, concentrate on the one point and strike and take it in the middle to drive it back and down into the water.

The fish.

The turtle.

Cold and strike and down, and he knew no more than that, knew no anger nor rage nor what he did nor why he did it. He knew nothing until he was in the lake, a scream-growl in his throat, in the lake holding Ray down to stop him, stop him, and the other two tearing at him, pulling at him.

"Stop it! Get off him! You'll kill him. . . ."

Tearing at him but not stopping him until Susan came to help, not to help him but to help the others get him away from Ray—Ray who was down in the water with the bubbles that were his life coming from his nose, bubbles coming up in a silver strand to carry his life up, up, up . . .

Then he was on the beach, sitting, dripping blood and water, his head between his knees, watching the blood and water from his face and hair dripping into the sand. Sitting still. Coming back. Susan stood next to him, her hand on his head, just touching his head. In front of him, vomiting, on his hands and knees, Ray crawled from the water with the other two boys helping him.

No talk for a time, a long time, his life. No talk. He didn't know who he was, where he was—just the line and the water and the last quarter of an inch, and the froth of scales and blood in the water. An end of something, an end of a fish, an end of what he had been and now something else new. But he knew nothing.

They helped Ray, still hacking and vomiting, into the boat and pushed it out. Wil stood watching the three boys ride away when the motor started—and still no talk, still no talk.

Then he sat again on the beach, trying to understand what had happened, looking at the water, just sitting. Susan sat next to him, said nothing, but now and again reached out to touch him. She had brought some toilet tissue for him, something he had not thought of, and she used a piece of it to dab at his face until the bleeding stopped. When the sun was nearly down, she said she had to go home, and he nodded, took her across in the boat; and when he turned the boat to row back, she said the first thing for that whole time. She said, "Wait. I'll come back tomorrow and bring you some aspirin."

He heard but did not say anything. He rowed back to the island and tipped the boat and started a fire and lay, staring into the flames, waiting for sleep to come.

But it did not come.

Only the cold thought was there, the cold thought that stayed until close to dawn, when it began to fade with the new light, and then, at last, he closed his eyes and slept.

THE TURTLE

By Wil Neuton

The turtle was wrong.

Maybe that's what got to me about what happened. Everything was working right and fitting in on the island and I could see how it was starting to work, work all right and the turtle was wrong.

Even the heron and the frog weren't the same. The frog died and fed the blue heron and that could be called wrong but it was different and didn't seem to be wrong. The heron fit the frog and the frog fit the heron and though there was death and the end of a thing, the end of the frog, it somehow fit and the turtle was wrong.

At first I thought it was that the fish was wrong. It was a young fish, a small and young sunfish and when it came to an end that was wrong and it made the turtle wrong. The sunfish had not made the quick circle and flash of gold the way they do when they get old and big and it had not had eggs or milt and it died, died before all that would come to be and that was wrong, I thought, and made the turtle wrong. But that's too easy a jump and it was something else, something else about the turtle that I could not see.

I thought of when the turtle came into the bay, all gray and dark and pointed and ugly with its hiss of breath, and how everything became quiet and still and of how the loons left. Left in fear. And how the fish left. Left in fear. And I thought that was wrong, the fear. The way the turtle came into the bay made me think of the way death came into my grandmother's life to take her and I thought maybe it was that which made the turtle wrong.

But that wasn't something the turtle controlled. The fear just came, and the loons just left, the fish just left, so it had to be something else still, some other thing.

The way the turtle killed the fish—slamming it sideways and the mess in the water with the fish curved tight and rigid in the turtle's beak, curved in death but not yet dead, curved to be swallowed but still not quite dead, that was wrong, a wrong end and I thought that made the turtle wrong.

But that wasn't something the turtle planned any more than he controlled the fear he caused when he came into the bay. So that couldn't be wrong, that couldn't be what was wrong with the turtle.

Then I thought of how it killed, quiet and deadly and waiting, waiting until the line had been crossed to kill, to smash and hammer and lunge and rip and tear and kill without thinking, without feeling and I thought that had to be it—that was what was wrong. That was why the turtle was wrong.

But why would it be better if he felt things? It wasn't the turtle's fault that he was cold-blooded, that he was a reptile, that he was what he was.

But the turtle was wrong.

I knew that. I know that.

And I would not have known still, would perhaps never have known if Ray hadn't come to the island. I tried to paint it, tried to know it from the way it had looked and that didn't work. But when Ray came . . .

No.

More than that. More than Ray coming to the island, although that was bad enough because when he came it was the same as the turtle coming to the bay to hit and slash and ruin. That was bad enough but that didn't make the turtle wrong any more than it made Ray wrong. Ray was just a bully and that's how bullies act and that was bad but that didn't make the turtle wrong.

It was the other thing. That's what finally came to me about the turtle. When Ray came to the island the turtle still wasn't wrong and when he mouthed off the turtle still wasn't wrong and when he hit me that way the turtle still wasn't wrong.

But when he crossed the line and went the last bit, the last inch and pushed or hit Susan and I became the turtle and the dark thing came from inside me— that's when the turtle was wrong.

The turtle was wrong because for that period of time that I couldn't remember well but knew only I was somehow part of the turtle I was wrong. The anger was wrong, the slashing, hitting thing I did was wrong, my rage was wrong and I was the turtle.

The turtle was wrong.

I was wrong.

17.

There are some things we aren't meant to do. It's sad, but that's just the way it is. I used to think I could do anything, or almost anything. But it just isn't so. I can't, for instance, learn to roller-skate. When it was really popular, I tried to learn. I went to the rink about fifteen times, maybe more, and I watched all the graceful skaters flitting around, and I wanted to be like them. But as soon as I let go of the boards, I left a grease spot on the rink. I'd crawl to the side and pull myself up, watch them for a few minutes, and then let go and make another grease spot when I splattered onto the floor. The only time I got going I found I couldn't turn and made a grease spot on the wall when I hit the end of the rink. I tried and tried and still never got to where I could do anything more than stand up. So there are some things we aren't meant to do. I can't spit to the moon and I can't roller-skate. Which might be why I wasn't popular in middle school. Who wants to hang around with somebody who keeps leaving grease spots on the rink?

—Wil Neuton

MORNING. Sun cooking down on the boat above him, heating the inside like a sauna. Wil opened his eyes and rolled stiffly out of the bag. He had slept hard, without moving, and his shoulders had taken a set.

He was ravenously hungry, and he found a can of fruit cocktail in the sack of food Susan had brought him. He opened it and drank the juice, then ate all the fruit, saving one small piece for the anthill. He walked over and put the piece of fruit down and sat to watch them for a few moments. The events of the previous day came with the ache in the side of his head, and he gingerly felt the cut over his cheek bone. It had started to scab over but still hurt when he touched it. What a strange thing, he thought, to want to fight that way— the way Ray wanted to. It proved nothing. Wil had had a few squabbles when he was small, but other than that there had not been trouble. As he'd said to Susan, he had learned early on to talk it over, talk it out.

And now he had fought, and now he had won. And for what? He wasn't sure what had happened to him, would try to think of it later and learn from it, but didn't like it—some kind of savage thing. And Ray had come close to getting drowned. For what?

He peeled off his clothes and went into the bay. After a small lap he rinsed his hair, let the cool water bring him up, then sat in the shallows in the soft sand, the water lapping across his stomach. Cool on the bottom, warm-hot on the top as the sun dried him.

My private bath, he thought. *The whole lake*. And no sooner was the thought out than he heard the water-buzzing sound of a motor starting again.

Probably Bunner coming back, he thought. *I need this. I really need Ray right now*. He felt a quick moment of anger mixed with sadness, then got out of the lake. He hand-wiped the water off and put his clothes on—

T-shirt, jeans. And shoes. If he had to fight again, he wanted shoes. He didn't want to fight, ever again, but he didn't want his feet bare if it happened.

Yet when the boat came around the point, it proved to be his parents, not Ray Bunner, and he had a sinking feeling as he saw how stiff his father was sitting at the motor. Rigid. With purpose.

He took the bow when they came in and helped pull the boat up. His mother took one look at him and nearly jumped out of the boat. "What happened to your face?"

Wil had forgotten the strike marks on his cheek and forehead. "Oh. Nothing. I fell on the rock while I was exercising. . . ."

"We're here to take you off this island." His father jumped right in—not this place, not take you home, not here to talk—take you off *this* island.

Wil shook his head. "I'm sorry. But I can't leave."

"What?"

And there it is, Wil thought. It had come to this—opposing thoughts, opposing minds. Opposite thinking. "I said I can't leave. Not yet. I am learning something, starting to know something about myself, about what I am. If I leave now, it will all be for nothing. I can't leave. Not yet."

"And what if I force you?" His father was barely controlling his anger. "I can do that—I can force you."

Wil studied him. He thought suddenly, insanely of the fight with Ray Bunner. *Force me*, he thought. *Why force me? Why all this talk of force?* "Maybe. I'm not sure, but maybe and maybe not. But Dad, think now, see it for what it really is. Why is it so bad that I want to stay here and learn?"

But another line had been crossed. His father, deep

in anger now, took a short step forward. "Because it's crazy. You're just a kid, a child. You have to be home with us to eat, to sleep, to be with your family. . . ."

"I eat here. I sleep here." And he almost added that his family was here but figured it wouldn't be a good time. "I'm healthy. I'm not doing anything wrong. I don't mean it as a challenge to you. I just want to stay here and learn and write and meditate. . . ."

"There's that word again, that cult word, *meditate*. That's another reason for you to leave." The words were getting louder, and Wil almost smiled because it sounded something like it did when his father worked on the plumbing. He wanted to fix his son, fix his problems with his son as he would a broken pipe. Scream and yell at it until it either was fixed or broken more.

"Dad. Mom. I don't think I'm crazy. But I know I have to stay here."

"How long?" his mother cut in. "How long would it take?"

"I don't know." He shrugged. "Until it's done."

"Until what's done?" His father now, hard still. Voice tight. "Until just exactly what is done?"

"Until I learn, understand, know more." *Fill the empty places*, he thought—*until I fill the empty places*. "Until it's done," he finished lamely.

"That's nuts. Just like I said, plain nuts. That's no reason to do anything. You can learn all that at home."

But now his mother studied him and held up a hand, one finger curved, and Wil had seen the curve before, couldn't remember when, then remembered suddenly that it was the same as his grandmother's finger, curving to point at something. The same finger. "You said you were writing and painting something. Could we see it?"

He thought about it, looked out across the lake, let his mind settle it. "I don't know. I kind of don't think so. It isn't really for seeing yet, I don't think. I guess I'd rather not."

"What's so secret about it?" His father climbed in. "Why can't we see it if it's so all-fired important?"

But before he could answer, his mother stepped forward. "That's all right, let it be. Listen, it's just that we don't understand and it frightens us. . . ."

"I'm not frightened," his father interrupted. "I'm not frightened at all. I'm just getting fed up."

"No wait, now wait. Listen, Wil, if we got somebody else out here to talk to you, somebody more . . . more professional about it all, would you mind that?"

Wil smiled. "You mean a shrink. You must really think I'm whacked-out if you want me to see a shrink."

"No, not at all. It's just that he might help us to understand it a little better. You know, understand about the island, why you're here. It's as much for us as anything. Would you mind?"

Wil shook his head. "No, not at all. If that's what you want, that's fine."

And she nodded and shushed his father, and they stayed a small time after that, but it was again all strained and tight. He showed them the island, where the turtle had hit, the anthill, how he was camping; but twice, out of the corner of his eye, he saw his mother whispering to his father, tight little whispers, and he tried to feel angry about it but couldn't. Instead he felt sad.

Sad for them. And when they left, he helped them off and waved, watched them wave back, and felt the sadness grow. It was a good-bye, somehow—a good-bye because they wanted to send the doctor.

161

He felt irritation then, for the coming doctor. He would be a bother. It would be impossible to work and learn while he was here, talking and talking.

Wil turned from them when they were out of sight. He wanted to write about Susan's mother, from what Susan had said, then about the fight—the fight and the thing that happened. He had to write of all that. There was a lot of work before the doctor came, a lot of work with new pencils and paint.

He took the notebook and sat on the rock, started working, concentrating. Working. The loons came back while he worked, checking the bay and staying when they found the turtle gone, talking and swimming near him; and he looked up, smiled at them, and went back to work.

SUSAN'S MOTHER

By Wil Neuton

She came to be in my mind in two ways, two different ways. But they both came out to be the same, the way two forks in a road both lead down to the same road and when I saw that, and felt that, I thought I should try to understand how it could be.

We sat at Susan's house in the kitchen and she brought us lunch, what they call dinner, and I didn't pay so much attention to her, the way you do with adults you've just met because usually they aren't all that interesting, but the light came in the kitchen window over the sink. It was a pale light because it came through the curtain and the curtain was yellow so it made the light gold, a pale yellow gold color that had little bits of dust riding in it and the light hit her face, hit Susan's mother's face, and set it to shining gold right at the cheekbone and up into her eyes.

It lighted her face to make it glow, and when she turned it moved into her hair, which was a gentle brown but turned into gold with the sun from the kitchen window and it was pretty, more than pretty, but still not so much. I saw it, but didn't think so much of it except that the light seemed to make her more than she was, maybe; set her off the way a frame sets off a painting.

But later at the island I saw the evening light

which was gold and it hit Susan, gold coming through the air hit Susan, and made her face shine and moved into her eyes and into her hair and it made me think of her mother, made her look like her mother.

No. That's not quite right. It wasn't that she looked like her mother so much as that she and her mother had the same . . . same core. The light hit them and made them the same. Not just made them look alike. But made them the same. I asked Susan to tell me about her mother so that I could write of her because if I write of her mother I may know Susan better. Not well enough, never well enough, but better.

And so Susan told me these things about her mother, and they are also of Susan because the light made them the same for me.

She was born in North Dakota and raised on a farm and had not been so happy with her life as a young girl. There were things Susan didn't know but a boy had come when she was a senior in high school and there was some trouble and she had run off with the boy. It hadn't worked and she'd come home but it was bad for her after being with the boy, and her father, Susan's grandfather, was too hard. When she got done with schooling she had gone. Just gone.

In southern Wisconsin she had taken work in a factory making farm equipment and had lived in an apartment with two other girls and had several boy-friends but none of them lasted. She'd told Susan about them but not in detail. Finally she'd quit the factory and taken another job in a brewery in Milwaukee and there she met Susan's father, who was off the farm they lived on now and had come to work in the factory long enough to get money to pay the banks off and not lose the farm.

They decided to work together and make more money faster and get back to the farm and that's what they did. They got married, the two of them alone, and saved their money and as soon as they could had come back north to the farm and had Susan's brother, then Susan, and that was the story Susan told about her mother.

Except.

Except that she was happy now and one time had not been happy and lived the way she wanted to now and at one time had not lived the way she wanted to. She had been two different people and I asked Susan what caused her to be that way, to find something that changed her and go with it, to be the way she wanted to be.

And Susan said it was her father. He had come along and they had fallen in love.

But that wasn't enough. That was part of what she became, I thought, and not reason for her to change—it was a result not a cause. And I thought again of what it could be in her that had made that, of what it could be in Susan that made her the same person. And in the end I could only guess, could only hope to see a tiny part of it.

It comes down to core.

The center of Susan's mother was her, was always

her, and when things didn't work right around the center she would change them but keep the center, keep the core. She and Susan had the same core. I think. The same center so that when the gold light hit them they were the same person because the gold somehow lighted the center of them, lighted the core of them.

And I thought that if I could know the center of her, of Susan's mother, then I would know Susan. So I tried but I think now it's something you can't do. You can't really know it but only try to know it and that's perhaps what living with other people is about, trying to learn the center of them, learn what they are, learn their core when they are in the golden dusty light of a kitchen window.

I thought then and think now that it would not be such a bad way to live, trying to understand Susan's mother by learning the center of Susan.

18.

Sometimes I fool myself into thinking things make sense when they really don't. I did that with work. We had this teacher who said we should all be able to grow up and get a job and work for our living when we finish with school. He was the kind of teacher who sold home products on the side and thought making money was what it was all about. The problem was that I liked him, so I thought he made sense. When I was in the eighth grade, I decided the best thing I could do is find a job and settle down, maybe get married later and have a good bank account. I worked on that for a while. Then spring came and a warm Saturday and the fish were running down at the dam and Petey came by with his bike, and the working and settling down didn't seem quite so important. Later I asked the teacher why the working was so important to him. He said so he could be secure. So why did he want to be secure? I asked. To have leisure time when he got old, he said. To do what? I asked. Well, he said, to go fishing. But I can go fishing now, I said. Which was the truth but might also explain why when I got him for economics next year I didn't get better than a C.

—Wil Neuton

SUSAN came later that afternoon, and he went for her in the boat. She brought some aspirin, as she had said, but most of the pain was gone, and he didn't take them. He was swollen and having trouble seeing out of his left eye now, but it didn't hurt much. She laughed and told him how word of his beating Ray would be all over the country by now—he'd be a hero— but Wil shrugged it off. It was not something he wanted to think about. He told her instead about his parents visiting him in the morning, some of it, most of it, and she smiled wistfully.

"Maybe you threaten them somehow."

"I can't see how. I just want to learn. And they're acting so . . . so different from how they are normally. We've always been loose, an easy family, and now they're all tight about this; I don't mean it as anything against them. I'm just trying to learn. . . . Maybe I'm wrong about staying out here like this. But I just can't turn it loose. It's the first thing in my life that's been this important to me."

He had been writing with the cedar pencils, writing of her mother, and she read it, and then more on the piece about the farmers, and she read that, shaking her head. "I know all these people, but I see them differently. You see things in them, places, what they are— it's fine, really fine, but I see them differently."

"I think everybody does." He nodded. "And everybody is right about everything, in a way. Because everything is different for everybody who sees it. Like when my mother was talking to me and pointing with her finger. She just wanted me to leave the island, and that's all she saw about what we were doing; she saw my dad's anger and the fact that she wanted me to leave the island. At the same time all I could see, all I could think about, was that her finger curved that way looked just like my grandmother's finger and hand used to look when she was pointing at the pictures to tell me about her life. That's all I could think about—they were the same, and I could see my grandmother in my mother and I could tell how my mother would look when she gets older. We were both right about what we saw, what we felt. And my father was right, too. . . ."

"Why didn't you let your parents read this, see this?" She held up the notebook. "You let me. It might have helped them to understand."

"I'm not sure. It just felt wrong. They didn't want to see it to learn about things, somehow. They wanted to use what I'd written to prove I was crazy so they could get me to leave. It was all negative. Too negative."

They stopped talking for a time then. He sat on the rock and worked, writing about the turtle and some more on Susan's mother, then some on his own mother. Susan walked the island and finally came and sat next to him, looking at the water. Once she reached over and touched his arm, just inside the elbow, and he looked up and smiled and still they said nothing; for an hour, another half hour, they sat next to each other. Then she stood and asked him to take her back to shore.

"So soon?"

She nodded.

"But why? I thought you were going to stay a while. . . ."

"I was, but I think I should go."

He waited, looking at her.

"Well." She took a breath. "This is changing now, that's all."

"What is?"

She swept her arm. "All of this, you, me. My mind is coming around on you, and the feelings just say maybe it would be better if I didn't come out to the island— well, you know."

So, Wil thought. *This is what my aunt was talking about. Love and things.* "I know. I feel it too."

"And if I stay or come out here again, you probably won't be learning much or working much, and we might get into some . . . problems. So I don't think I should stay out here with you."

"But when it's done . . ."

"Nothing. Don't say anything. We'll see what happens then. Now, will you take me back to shore?" She sighed, then blew the hair up out of her eyes, and he thought he had never seen anything so pretty, but he said nothing. She was right. They could have some trouble. *Pretty soon, too,* he thought. *In fact . . .*

"I'll take you back now." He turned the boat and dragged it with her help into the water. "I'll take you back. . . ."

They said nothing while he rowed, didn't need to say anything. When they got to shore, she leaned from her seat to his and kissed him, gently on the mouth, softly, then stepped out of the boat and onto the grass and smiled at him. "You're a good friend."

"Thank you. So are you."

"I'll bring some more food in a day or two and just hand it to you here."

"Thank you." *That's me,* he thought—*Mr. Conversation.* "I'm not saying things right, not saying them the way I want to say things to you. I want to say more than thank you, but I don't think it's time, is it?"

"No, not yet."

Then she said good-bye, twice, and he said it twice and watched her walk to her bike, wheel it onto the road, and start riding. He watched until she was gone from sight among the trees, and still he watched where she had last been, watched and watched before he finally pulled back to the island.

That night it was strange. Stranger than it had been. He felt utterly, completely, almost viciously alone. *Alone on earth*, he thought, staring at the fire after he had eaten a can of stew. The mosquitoes were particularly bad. He doped up with repellent, but they seemed to lick it off, so he got a handful of green leaves and threw one or two of them on the fire every few minutes. The dense cloud of smoke from the green leaves kept them away, and he had time to think.

Alone. He was somehow more apart from his parents than he had ever been because they were so against what he was doing. Alone from his family. Alone from his parents. Alone from what he knew. And with Susan gone, alone from friendship, alone from companionship.

Alone on earth, he thought again. *I might as well be the only person left on the planet.* And when that thought was upon him, at the height of his loneliness, the loon cried.

It was not the first time she'd cried at night. In fact every night she made some songs—sweet sounds that he heard but didn't really hear at all, sounds that floated over him. But this night, this time when he was alone in his mind, the moon came up full over the water, cut a silver path across the surface of the lake that flooded from the sky into him; and she sat in the middle of this white path, sat in the middle and cried a new song, a keening new high song that came from the moon and into him.

The song was so rich, so sweet and pure, that it stopped him, stopped all of what he was thinking, and he stood next to the boat, stood and saw her sitting out in the moonlight and could not, would never know what the song meant but knew that if he could capture the sound, the cutting of the sound, for any feeling in his life it would fit. It would fit joy and peace, anger, love..

She did it three times, sat in the moonlight and started low, with almost inaudible raspings, an earthy sound that slid up into the high keen, the pure sound that hung in the night, hung in the moonlight, hung in his mind and soul, and then she was done. Three times and done.

He went to the rock, everything forgotten but the sound, stood there for the last one, the last cutting wail, and let it hold him. When he was sure she was finished, he tried the sound, tried starting low and lifting his voice, but he couldn't make it pure enough, not even close.

He tried several times but could not do it, could not do it. His throat didn't work correctly for the sound, neither his throat nor his mouth nor somehow his mind. Yet he felt that if he could capture the sounds of the loon, not all of them but just this sound that came down the moon-white slash on the water—if he could know that sound, he could know all of music. All of sound.

But it escaped him, and he went back to the fire, where he lay on his bag, still feeling completely alone, staring at the coals. He could not write it, he could not paint it—he couldn't make the sound. Perhaps, he thought, with an instrument he could duplicate the cutting edge of the sound. But he didn't know what kind of instrument, and what it came down to, finally, was that he could not learn this sound.

You had to be a loon, he thought, to make this sound. You had to understand all that a loon understood, be all that a loon could be, go all the places a loon could go—you had to be a loon.

And so, he thought, dozing, *maybe it's that way with all things. Perhaps you cannot learn, truly learn of something unless you become what you're trying to understand*— as he could write about the turtle because he became, finally, when he fought Ray, something very close to the turtle.

But how then, he thought, *how to write of or paint anything except yourself?*

How could you become your grandmother?

A long and strange night.

19.

*One day about four of us were sitting during the lunch hour
outside—we bring lunches because the cafeteria food is not be-
lievable and what do they put in those "nuggets" anyway?—
and we decided to figure out what made a dirty word dirty. We
threw a few of them back and forth, the way you do, and said
them to each other, but they didn't seem dirty. After a while we
decided that no word is dirty if you don't want it to be and the
best way to stop it from being bad is to stand alone somewhere
and say the dirtiest word you know aloud over and over—
maybe for fifteen or twenty minutes. By the time you said a
dirty word that many times alone, to yourself, it wouldn't be
dirty any longer. It would just be boring. But Frank Kline said
he wasn't going to do it because the dirtiest word he knew was
actually two words and he wasn't going to stand for twenty
minutes saying "greasy salve" over and over. Turns out he had
a skin condition when he was a kid, and they kept rubbing this
greasy salve on him, and he still thinks it's the dirtiest thing
there is. Greasy salve. How could you look at somebody and
say, "Oh, go to greasy salve." Dirt is definitely in the eye of the
beholder. Or as Frank said, there are dirters and dirtees, and it
isn't dirty unless the dirtee says it is.*

—Wil Neuton

"Hello." The voice came from the beach just as Wil was thinking about getting up. He had finally dozed just before dawn, and the sun hitting the boat had awakened him. "Anybody home?"

Woman's voice, he thought. *Strange woman. Probably the shrink. That was sure fast.* He thought it would take at least a couple of days for his mom and dad to find a psychiatrist out here in the sticks. *Ahh, well, why not?*

"I'll be right out," he said from beneath the boat, pulling on his pants, "as soon as I get dressed." *I feel like a troll*, he thought, *living under this boat.* He had a mental image of a wiry little man with a peaked cap and a beard living under old boats, wearing old leather clothes. *Some kind of hobbit. A troll.*

He crawled out from under the boat and thought that this was an awkward way to meet a psychiatrist. Crawling at her feet. *No, I'm not crazy, and I live under this boat and crawl around on the beach.* He stood up, brushed the sand off his knees and smiled. "Overslept. I had a late night. I didn't figure you'd come for at least another day."

"You didn't?" She was tall, with brown hair and long arms that were graceful-looking. He couldn't tell age on adults, but maybe thirty or forty or so. Older woman. But she had a nice smile and a tanned face. In back of her, pulled up on the sand, was a sixteen-foot canoe with a paddle across the front seat. The woman was wearing jeans and a T-shirt and a cap that had a picture of a bass jumping on it. She had a shoulder-pack, which she took off and put down on the sand.

"You were expecting me?" She looked puzzled. "How

strange. I didn't know myself I was coming until last night. . . ."

"My folks said they were going to get you—or get someone. I just thought it would take more time. I didn't know they could get a doctor on such short notice."

"Doctor?" She laughed. "Not likely. You've got me confused with somebody else. Although I would like to know why you need a doctor—for that mess on your face?" She stepped forward and held out her hand. "My name is Anne Kelliher. I'm kind of a reporter, and I'm here to interview you and find out what this is all about."

"A reporter?"

"Well, sort of. I work for the Pinewood *Caller*—I didn't name the paper. I do advertising selling, writing, editing—most of it. But I also do stories, which appear in a whole series of small northern newspapers, along with the *Caller*. And that's why I'm here. I heard about you and thought you might make a good story."

"Heard what?"

"Nothing detailed. Just about the boy who wouldn't leave the island and then a little about the problem you had with Ray Bunner."

"You know about Ray Bunner?"

"Everybody knows about Ray Bunner. Although I hear he's settled a bit since he came out here. You must have put the fear into him."

"No. I didn't mean to, anyway. It's just something that . . . happened. That's all. Not a big thing."

"Would you mind if we did an interview? And if I took some pictures?" She held up her bag. "There's a camera and tape recorder in here."

Wil thought about it, rubbed the back of his neck. On

the one hand he seemed to be getting a lot of people involved in something he was trying to do alone. It started alone, but now there were Susan and his parents and Ray and, of all things, a reporter. "I don't know. . . ."

She smiled, open and genuine. "I won't push it if you don't think it would be right. But maybe if we talk, just talk, and you explain to me what you're doing out here, we can see if it's going to be a story or not. Sometimes things that seem interesting for stories don't pan out, and sometimes they seem wrong and come out right."

"I know. I tried to do the loon song and it didn't come out right for me, and when I tried to write the song it didn't work. . . ." He stopped. She was watching him with interest, her face slightly puzzled, but not pushing. Perhaps if he talked it over with her, just talked, he could understand more of what was happening with his mind.

"Maybe that would be best. I mean what we have here, on the face of it, is a perfectly normal fifteen-year-old boy who has always been pretty level suddenly going whacko and trying to learn things on an island."

"I don't think you're whacko. Not at all. But let me start my recorder first. Then if we don't like it, I'll leave the tape with you and that's the end of it. On the other hand, if it works out I'll have it. All right?"

He nodded. She turned on the recorder and brought out an omnidirectional mike, and they sat in the sand. "Just let it come," she said. "I might ask a question now and then, but you talk about anything you want."

Again he nodded but was silent. The mike stopped him for a moment. "I can't think how to start. . . ."

"Just begin with the first time you came out here. Start with that and let it come. What brought you to the island?"

Wil frowned, thinking. A fly came in close, and he waved it away. "Well, let's see. I was riding my bike and I came on this lake and there was the boat, an old minnow boat, and I saw the island sitting out there alone, this island, so I got the boat going and took the old oars. . . ."

And he was into it and gone and talking. He couldn't stop. It seemed the more he told her, the more he wanted to tell her and the more he wanted to find out. Things came to him as he talked, things he didn't know he knew; they flowed out of him, flowed out of him as if he were writing or painting or moving to learn. Before he knew what or why, he had taken out the notebook and paintings and showed them to the reporter, showed them all except the paintings of Susan when she'd been swimming, and Anne took pictures of them, pictures of the notebook, of the watercolors. At one point he went to the rock and moved, did the dance of the heron, did his exercises and she took pictures of all of it.

All of it.

When at last he was done, tired, sitting again on the sand and done, he had told her not just about the island but about his life, about what he was, what his parents were, his grandmother. He had told her all that he was, all that he knew, and when he stopped it happened just that way. He stopped. He was talking about Ray Bunnis coming out, and he didn't know how that happened, so he stopped.

Anne Kelliher sat across from him, by the dead fire, the recorder still going, her mouth half open. Stunned.

"So . . ." Wil smiled. He was hoarse from talking and run-out in his mind. "So. Am I whacko?"

She said nothing, still staring at him, her forehead

wrinkled in a frown. At last she shook her head. Slightly at first, then with more emphasis. "No. No. No. I don't . . . I don't know what to say. This is astounding . . . something. I don't know what has happened to you, but I know you're not crazy. You're doing, you're doing, you're doing something . . . I don't know. I don't know what to say."

"Is there a story there?"

"Story? Is there a story there? Listen, this . . . what's happened to you is special, is wonderful and special. I think it's really something, somehow it's something we all want to do—we all want to find an island and learn all we can about all we are. It's more than a story. You've found something . . . I don't know. But I do know it's a story. The pictures, what you said, the writing, all of it. It might be a great story, and I hope you let me do it."

And he did. Without thinking he told her to go ahead and do it, and she nodded and turned to leave, slid her canoe out. Just as she jumped in, she turned to him. "Listen. Don't worry about the doctor. Just tell him what you told me and you'll be all right."

She was gone, gliding across the bay with smooth strokes of the paddle. He watched her until the canoe silently disappeared around the corner of the island; then he found wood and started a fire. Night was coming and the mosquitoes, and he wanted to write more of what he had learned while talking to her, more on the grandmother piece, and he felt serene and happy.

There was not a single indication of the storm he'd just unleashed.

20.

There are things you can't think about because your brain
won't work the right way. Petey and Frank and I were sitting
watching the football team turn to meat, and Petey said that
when he died he wanted to come back as a coach to get even
with all the jocks. That got us to thinking about it, and we decided that it didn't do any good to think about what happened
after you were dead because you wouldn't know it. You might
come back as a bird or anything, and you would never know
you'd been a kid, so what good did it do to think about it? It's
not something the brain works right for doing. Which doesn't
mean much but that's how we spent our afternoons sometimes.

—Wil Neuton

His parents didn't find "professional help"
right away. All the next day Wil was alone, and he got
up and meditated and did his exercises, stretching the
muscles that had been somehow hurt when he fought
Ray—or didn't fight Ray. Did what he did with Ray.
He didn't think of it as a fight.

But he pulled the muscles out and tried the loon call
and ate some rolls that Susan had put in the bag. The

rest of the day he spent painting, scenes of the lake and the island, a try at fish under water, hiding under rocks, a try at the turtle again—to write of it and paint it, and how he had been with Ray—but he still couldn't remember enough. All day working hard, never quite getting what he wanted but learning, learning all the time and pushing his thoughts out ahead of him so he had to struggle to keep up with them.

In the late afternoon Susan yelled from the shore, and he rowed in to find that she had a small bag of food for him and a rain poncho—he had brought nothing for rain. She said little, but when their eyes caught each other they could not look away for a full five seconds and so said much without words. She left as soon as he had the food in the boat, and he rowed back to the island.

It clouded toward evening, and the darkness came rapidly, then a light rain, but he sat under the boat and worked in the firelight. He had pulled some broken pieces of driftwood in under the boat as well and put them on as the wood burned out, listening to the raindrops sizzle and hiss when they hit the coals and flames. He tried to paint the flames, but it didn't work; and he wondered if it was because they were always moving, kind of painting themselves, the flames, and it didn't work to paint a painting just as it didn't work to write about something that is written.

Sleep almost rolled over him, and he slid down into the bag and went under watching the fire, as he'd done before, and thought how he could probably fall asleep watching a fire for the rest of his life and not be bored by it.

Morning.

No sun this time. Clouds hung down, low, almost on the lake it seemed, and they let go with a steady misting drizzle that turned everything the same gray, flat color. The fire was dead, ashes gray-dead like the sky, dead and wet and cold, and he wanted to stay in the bag all day but knew that wouldn't work. He unzipped and crawled out but stayed under the boat in a crouch while he ate a can of pears and drank the juice.

Food helped. He took out the paints and worked on a painting of the gray day, the gray fire, all in blacks and blacks diluted into grays, and it worked, it worked. It wasn't all that he wanted, but it worked. And he started another, a painting of the anthill in the rain, wondering how the ants took care of the rain, and that painting was working, was on the point of working, when he heard the steady *thunk-thunk* of a small outboard. He looked from under the boat—*a troll*, he thought, *I'm still a troll*—to see an aluminum boat pulling into the bay and up to the beach.

There was one man in the boat, and he was wearing a bright orange rain jacket and a bright orange cap that covered his head down to his ears. He was a heavy man, very round, and Wil thought he looked like a bright orange doughboy as he stepped backward out of the boat and turned.

I don't, Wil thought, *have enough orange paint in both boxes to handle this one. There isn't enough orange paint in the world.*

"Hi," the stranger said, smiling. He had a mustache, and it drooped in the rain but wiggled on the ends when he smiled. *Like two hairy bats*, Wil thought. "My name is Weaver. Charles Weaver. But everybody I know just calls me Chuck."

"You're the doctor." *It had to be*, Wil thought. *A doctor named Chuck. A psychiatrist named Chuck. I'd like you to meet my shrink, Chuck.* He almost said, "What's up, Chuck?" but decided it would not be a good way to start off with a doctor.

"No. No. Well, sort of, maybe. I'm a professional counselor, and your parents asked me if I would come out here and . . . talk to you a bit. About why you're on the island. Would you share that with me?"

"Share what?"

"Share your feelings with me."

Here is the troll, Wil thought, *peering out from under his old turned-over boat on the magic mushroom island, staring up at an orange marshmallow standing in the rain who wants to share feelings.* "Would you like to sit under the boat?"

"Would you like me to sit under the boat?"

Oh, Wil thought, *one of those. The kind who answer questions with a question.* He'd had one of those in seventh grade, a counselor who did the questions. They called him The Question Mark and, finally, just The Mark. He was all right, Wil remembered, and tried. But the kids couldn't talk to him because he never said anything. Just asked questions. "Sure. If you want to sit under the boat, sit under the boat."

"But would you feel all right with that?"

"With what?"

"With me sitting under the boat. I don't want to invade your space if you don't want me to. Will you feel all right with that?"

It probably wouldn't do any good, Wil thought, *to scream at him. He'd just think I was nuts, never knowing that he was the reason I'm nuts.* He wondered for a second, watching the rain drip down on the orange man with the drooping mustache, just how many times people were fine until they met the counselor or shrink and then they went whacko. "I wouldn't mind at all," he said in measured, slow tones, "if you want to sit under the boat. I'm all right with that."

"Fine then. If you're all right with that, I'm all right with your being all right with it. I'll come under the boat."

He stooped and crawled in, his huge orange bulk completely filling the end of the boat opposite Wil. "This is really neat," he said, relating, he thought, to Wil. "Just like camping out in the Boy Scouts, eh?"

Wil nodded but didn't say anything. The man meant well, but he was so far off the track about what was happening there was almost no way for Wil to explain anything to him. Not so he could understand. It was kind of sad because the one thing he was out here for was to understand Wil and there was not a chance that he could, not the way he was going. It was the same with his father. And there was no reason for him to expect anything different, really. His parents had hired this man to talk him off the island, so why would he try to understand? He wasn't being paid to understand. He was being paid to make Wil come home.

"Why don't you want to be with your parents?" Weaver asked suddenly. "Is it because they won't give you something you want? Is that why you're fighting them on this? Staying out here?"

Turtle, Wil thought. *Oh, I have seen the turtle do that*

under the rock, do that with the fish, and I have seen the blue heron standing still in the shallow water against the dawn sky waiting for the water to move, waiting for food to move, and I have heard the loon in the silver moonlight across the flat water, and all of this you think is because my parents won't give me something. There is not a way, Wil thought, *not a way for this man to understand what is happening with me.* "No. It isn't that. I don't want anything. In fact . . ." Wil was going to say that he loved his parents and liked to be with them, but Weaver cut him off.

"I must say there is no external evidence of drug use," the orange round man said, "but that doesn't always mean anything. It can be easily hidden."

Wil started to lose his patience, held it. "I don't use drugs. Never have and hope I never do."

Weaver said nothing for a moment, sat at the other end of the boat, studying Wil like some kind of specimen or experiment. At last he sighed. "There is no indication of abuse. . . ."

"Enough." Wil snapped. "Enough of this now. My parents are loving, helpful people who have never abused me and who try hard to take good care of me. I am not here because something out there is bad; I'm here because something here is good. I'm here because when I came I started to learn something about myself, about . . . about things, and I want to know more. My parents are having trouble understanding that, that's all. That's absolutely all."

Again Weaver sat silently, studying him. Then he shook his head. "Of course you would say that even if you were being abused. Sometimes the abusee will try to hide it. . . ."

"Arrrgh!" Wil yelled his frustration. "Read my lips. I . . . am . . . not . . . being . . . abused . . . by . . . anybody. I am not being abused and I am not taking drugs and I am not in trouble with school and I am not having any other kind of difficulty at home or in my life. Do you understand?"

Weaver frowned, thinking. The frown made the mustache droop still more, and for a moment he resembled nothing so much as a large, frowning walrus sitting under a boat in a bright orange jacket. Drops of moisture slid from the hairs of the mustache and dropped onto his arm. "Let me get this straight," he said. "You're telling me that nothing negative is happening to you— is that right?"

Except you, Wil thought. But he held his tongue and nodded. "Nothing negative is happening to me. Nothing."

"So this doesn't require a negative therapy approach."

Whatever that is, Wil thought. But again, he didn't say it. "No, this doesn't require a negative therapy approach."

Weaver thought some more, the mustache wiggling and drooping. "So what we might be dealing with is a neutral therapy approach requirement, or"—his voice broke with excitement—"or . . ."

I have to ask, Wil thought, *just to be polite.* "Or what?"

"This just might be a positive therapy approach requirement—a P.T.A.R. We just might be dealing with a P.T.A.R. situation."

"So what does that mean?"

Wiggle, droop, drip. Then, in a hushed voice under the dark boat on the gray day, Weaver said in a reverent voice, "I've never had this situation before, so I'll have to read up on it. But I think it means that you're reacting to there being nothing wrong with your life. We'll have to treat that. . . ."

"Wait a minute." Wil held up his hand. "Are you telling me that you're going to counsel me because there's nothing wrong?"

"Well, like I said, I'll have to read up on it. But that's what it looks like, yes. We'll have to treat you for . . ."

"For nothing being wrong."

Weaver nodded. "Yes. Exactly. We'll have to develop a therapy line for no problem—you might call it a zero effect therapy line."

Maybe I am crazy, Wil thought. *I think I'm starting to understand him.* "So what you're telling me is that because nothing is wrong you're going to counsel me with a form of therapy that doesn't do anything—is that right?"

Again Weaver nodded. "It's incredible. I may be written up in the journals for this one."

I have to try it, Wil thought. "What about if you didn't counsel me at all?"

Weaver brightened, thought about it for a moment, then shook his head. "No. That wouldn't work. I've been retained to counsel you, and I have to counsel you—there are ethics involved."

"Yes, of course. I see now." Wil nodded. "Silly of me to miss it in the first place."

"No problem. You couldn't know—it's a professional consideration. Well—" Weaver slapped his hands on his legs—"it's been a fruitful session, don't you agree?"

"Very."

"I'll go away and read up on this, and we'll have

another go in two or three days. Will you still be here?"

"Yes. I think so."

"Fine, then. Just fine." Weaver clambered out from under the boat and stood in the drizzle, adjusted the orange rain jacket to straighten the hood on his head. "Just fine . . ." He started to walk away, toward his boat on the sand.

"Mr. Weaver?" Wil stuck his head out and peered up. "Mr. Weaver, if it's not against ethics, would you tell me what you're going to tell my parents?"

The counselor stopped, scratched his mustache. "No, I don't see any ethical problem with telling you. It might even help, you know, help you. When I get back, I'll tell your parents that absolutely nothing is wrong"— he turned and grabbed the bow of his boat—"and that we're doing everything we can to help you through it."

And they think I'm *crazy*, Wil thought, watching him pull on the cord until the motor started and Weaver rumble-thunked out of sight. *And they think* I'm *crazy*.

21.

I used to have a lot of problems with deciding value. My dad said it all depended on price tags. A new garden tiller that cost three hundred dollars was worth three hundred dollars. But one day Petey was batting rocks with a stick, just throwing them up and hitting them, and he put a rock accidentally through old man Grotchaw's window, which would have cost about seven dollars to fix. But Mr. Grotchaw came after Petey at a dead run, and Petey panicked and ran through the Peterson's yard, where Mrs. Peterson had her laundry hung. Petey caught his neck on Peterson's clothesline, did a complete backflip, got tangled in her laundry, and ran into her open basement doorway wrapped in sheets and towels. Their sewer had backed up, and they had the basement door open to dry it out. Petey hit the slippery floor and mess, and by the time he got out of there— sounding like a herd of water buffalo—he didn't know where he was and had trouble saying his own name. If you were to tell Petey it was all because of a seven-dollar window, he'd think you were crazy. Petey claims it changed his life. It might be that value depends on whether or not you hit Mrs. Peterson's clothesline at a dead run—I don't know.

—Wil Neuton

Hᴇ worked hard after Weaver left, tried to paint the gray-rain day, tried to write of Weaver but kept smiling when he thought of the orange man sitting under the boat. Most of the day Wil sat on his bag, listening to the rain, touching up the other work he had done. In late afternoon the sun came out, and he stood and stretched and thought he saw a flash of light on the shoreline, opposite the end of the island.

It was an odd flash, not like a fire but brighter. Perhaps the flash of sunlight on a mirror or . . .

Binoculars?

He studied the shoreline where the flash had appeared but saw nothing. No movement, no sign of anything. After a time he began to believe he had imagined it and went about his business. His bag was dampish, and he aired it, opened over a poplar branch. Then he gathered more driftwood from the windward side of the island and brought it back in the boat. The evening would be muggy, warm, and without rain; the mosquitoes would flock on him, and he wanted to have plenty of wood to keep a small smoke-fire going. Just as he was putting the last piece of wood down by the boat, he thought he caught the flash again, from the same place.

He crouched in back of the boat, out of line of sight to the flash point and waited, hidden except for one eye that peered around the corner of the stern. For a long time there was nothing; then he saw the flicker of light again and right after that a movement of blue that might have been jeans.

Then nothing. He waited and watched for a full ten minutes, sitting very still, but saw nothing more.

It can't be Susan, he thought. *She would wave or call. It might be Weaver—"studying" him. Or maybe Bunner and those guys, spying on him, trying to catch him doing something weird.* He watched for a time more but finally decided it didn't matter who it was; he still had things to do. He went back to work—cleaning up the camp, gathering rocks to put around his fire pit—and ignored whoever it was on the shore. Twice more he caught bits of light, in the afternoon, but he didn't pay any attention.

Just at evening he walked the beach one more time and found the almost bare skeleton of a dead sunfish washed up and into the sand. At first he thought it might be the body of the one killed by the turtle but then realized it was much older. Just the bones and the hard outer shell of the skull carapace. It was so old it didn't smell, and he kneeled over it, studying it.

He had seen many dead fish, but this one was different. He couldn't at first pin it down, but there was a difference with it, some new oldness that he didn't understand. There was a curve to the spine and all the side bones, ribs, as they curved down into the sand. . . .

Into the sand. That was it. The fish skeleton had drifted in, and the lapping of the small waves had buried part of the tail in fine sand, beach sand, covered it so the curve of the spine down into the sand almost made the fish body look planted. It was as it the fish was not truly dead, was indeed alive and of the earth.

The fish had only changed. *But more, not just the fish, but more now*, he thought—*more and more as I learn this, as I learn me* . . . not just the fish changes when it dies but doesn't die. Not just the fish. Maybe all things, maybe all things only change, only come from the earth a different way when they die. If he could know this, know about the fish and the curve from the earth, from the sand up into the skeleton—perhaps if he knew that, he could know of death.

Perhaps then he could understand his grandmother more.

So he worked to write of the fish as it became dark. Once more, just at dusk, he stood to stretch and do exercises and match the curve of the fish, match the curve that came from the sand up the spine of the fish and into all of life somehow; and just then he thought he caught the flash again of the setting sun on the shoreline where it had flickered before, but he didn't care. If somebody wanted to watch, he could watch. He had to write of the fish and the earth and the curve.

It took him some time because the wood was still damp, but he at last got a fire going and sat the rest of the evening into hard dark writing and trying to paint the fish from memory, and when at last he went to sleep he knew some of it but not enough, not yet enough.

Dawn. It came early, as it always did in the north in the summer: first true light in June about four in the morning, sun up shortly after that, birds singing.

Wil wasn't sure what awakened him. He had worked until well after midnight by the fire, and he figured to sleep a little late. But something awakened him just at dawn, and he didn't know what.

What he did know was that as soon as his eyes were open and he was awake, he heard a muffled series of thumps and bumps, out of sight in the bay, then mumbled whispering and some mild swearing.

For a second he thought he might still be asleep and dreaming it all. But the bird songs kicked in and grew deafening, and he knew the thumps and whispers were real. He was truly awake, and he slid sideways and peeked out around the end of the boat. He couldn't believe what he saw and rubbed his eyes to look again.

In the bay there were three boats, side by side. They had outboard motors but they also had oars and they must have been rowed, Wil thought, or he would have heard motors. At first they seemed to be crawling with men, all holding equipment and cables and packs full of things, mumbling and whispering at each other. But in a few seconds Wil could see that each boat held three men, and one man in each boat was holding a portable television camera, while the other two were holding battery packs and extra supplies.

Wil ducked back under the boat and unzipped his bag. This was absolutely crazy.

"He's up," he heard one of them whisper. "I saw movement. He's up. Get ready to catch him when he comes out. We want it all natural, all like he doesn't know we're here."

Wil rolled out, stood and stretched. Then he smiled at them and waved. "Good morning . . ."

"No. No. Don't wave. We just want you to act natural—just do what you do."

Wil squinted at them. The sun was slightly in back of them, and he caught the light in his eyes. "Who are you?"

"We're television news teams from Madison and Milwaukee."

"What? What do you mean? Television . . ."

"Kid, you're famous. That newspaper story was picked up by the news wire. 'The Kid on the Island' is all over the place. We're here to cover your story. Now just act natural."

Great, Wil thought. *Just great. La, la. And I have to go to the bathroom—that might be a little too "natural" for them.* "Could you turn the cameras off?"

"Why?"

"Just for a minute . . ."

They finally got it. "Oh, sure."

The one who had been speaking was in the center boat, but now the rest of them started asking questions. "How long have you been here? What are you protesting against? When did you realize that you were different from other children? How old are you? Why are you being 'The Kid on the Island?' " And on and on, a flood of questions that mixed and mixed into a mess until he couldn't hear them individually at all but only as a porridge . . . a slop.

He turned his back on them and tried to think. This wasn't going to work. If they kept on him, he wouldn't be able to get anything done. But what could he do? He took out a can of peaches and opened them, to the sound of the zoom motors on the cameras humming as they taped him. It had been a mistake to do the story with Anne, that was for sure. He thought as he ate, silently, and it came down to just two ways he could go. He could either sit and do nothing, which would bore them and they would probably leave, or he could "act natural" and give them what they wanted, in which case they might leave. He finished the peaches and took the juice and a small bit up to the ants; then he turned to the men in the boat.

"All right. I can't do much with you guys around— I'd get too involved with what you're doing. So if I answer your questions and let you take some pictures, would you leave me to myself?"

They haggled among themselves in the boat for a bit—Wil smiled because they looked like a bunch of crows sitting in a tree yelling at each other—but at last they agreed.

"If you'll give us enough for a good story, we'll take off," the spokesman said. "but you have to give us enough."

Wil nodded. "I'll tell you what I'm doing here, everything, and you can tape what you want." *Then I'll have some peace*, Wil said to himself. "But you might as well come to shore. There's a lot of stuff you'll have to get close up."

"We didn't want to bother you. . . ."

Right, Wil thought, watching them come to the beach and pull the boats up. *You didn't want to bother me, right. Well, we might as well get to it.* He dug out his notebook and the watercolor of the dead fish and walked over to the skeleton sticking out of the sand on the beach.

The camera crews clambered out of their boats and followed him, taping as they came. The three announcers held out their mikes, watching him, waiting. When he came to the fish he stopped and pointed down. "There."

The cameras turned down to the fish.

"There what?" the man who had spoken in the boat asked.

"There is one of the things I am doing here. . . ."

All of the cameras swung up to his face as Wil began, then back down to the fish. It was like talking to three one-eyed monsters. The announcer bent over, looked at the fish closely, pinched his nose and looked back to Wil. "You're out here playing with rotten, dead fish?"

Wil shook his head. "No. See now, look at it—see how the curve comes up from the sand, as if it's not dead at all but growing up from the earth again. The curve of the spine, see, and the shape of the angle to the sand, and it all makes something else, something that comes alive. . . ."

And they nodded, and they filmed the dead fish, and they smiled; but Wil could see that they didn't understand, and that was his fault, not their fault, his fault because he said it wrong for them. He showed the painting and tried to tell them about what he would write of the fish, then felt the dam go down, the wall, and he told them all of it.

He talked for over two hours, showing them all of it except the paintings of Susan swimming, and they taped it. The three of them taped it all and followed him all over the island, saw the anthill and where the turtle hit the fish and where the problem with Ray had happened; and Wil could see them change, could see them take it in. In the end he went out on the flat rock and showed them the heron, the moves that made the heron, not to show off but because the moves were part of the writing and part of the painting and part of what was happening to him.

When he was done, it was close to midmorning, the sun well up, and he caught the flash of light on the shore again, and the roll of blue from somebody's jeans.

Whoever it was, he or she was persistent. The three camera crews were silent but not with the silence of waiting so much as the silence of thought. Wil shrugged. "Well. That's it. That's why I'm here."

The spokesman sighed. "It's like she said in the article—kind of incredible. I mean we're out here taping things and doing things and we're missing it—missing something . . ."

Wil smiled. "Go find an island."

They climbed into their boats, but as the last cameraman started to step over the gunwale, Wil stopped him. "That camera has a zoom telephoto, doesn't it?" Wil had played with video cameras and zoom lenses in Madison in school and recognized the big lens.

"Sure does . . ."

"Can I see through it?"

"Sure. No problem."

The camerman unshouldered the camera and settled it on Wil's shoulder. Wil stuck his eye in the rubber eyepiece and put his finger in the zoom trigger-button. He scanned back and forth a couple of times on the lake, then centered on the shore and pulled the trigger to enlarge the spot where he'd seen the flash of light and bit of blue. It was easy to see the figure of a man squatting at the base of a tree with a pair of old army-surplus binoculars to his eyes, looking at Wil.

Wil had begun to suspect it, but when he saw the familiar figure sitting there watching him—watching him all the previous day and all the night and all this day—when he saw the man, his heart went out across the lake to him.

Hello, he thought, looking through the zoom lens.

Hello, Dad.

22.

*Trying to do things right can get you in corners. I remember
once in math class in the seventh grade Frank Kline, who is one
of those people who do math well, proved the teacher was
wrong. I don't remember what the problem was, but he proved
the teacher was wrong and that might have been the right thing
to do but it was also the wrong thing to do. Frank got to say he
was right, but he spent the rest of the year with old Laser Eye
Mitchell, the math teacher, watching him like a hawk. Frank
figured it was the most uncomfortable hour-each-day-for-a-full-
school-year that he had ever spent, and he couldn't do any of
those things you do to get through math—like notes or rub your
nose or hold your breath. "It was a lot of strain," he said
later, "just to be right. I might have developed a nervous skin
condition." Which is the sort of thing Frank worries about.*

—Wil Neuton

Wil watched the three boats leave, which
was, he thought, a lot like seeing one of those Hun-
garian circus acts in which everybody is jumping around
and yelling. The three camera crews and announcers

jumped and yelled in the boats, got their oars tangled, got untangled, more yelling and screaming and near disasters and, finally, they were out of sight. Wil heard them for some time as they made their way across the lake.

At last even the sound was gone, and he sat on the flat rock in the sun to think. They had taped it all, and that should be the end of it, unless they somehow thought of something else to ask. But he couldn't imagine that—the press made one hit and got bored, went on to something else. They would cover the first part of something but rarely follow it up. You almost never heard or saw on television how things turned out, just how things started.

They were gone now.

And, he thought, looking at the water by his legs, where the turtle had been, *and how will this turn out? And . . .*

He went back to the boat and found the notebook and sat with one of the cedar pencils and a blank page, sat staring at nothing, thinking and not thinking—almost being and not being. He thought of the turtle, of Susan, of the sun, the camera crew, the island—and he could have written of any of them, could have painted any of them; but when it came, when it came to him, the pencil moved and he had written:

MY FATHER.

Just in that way, all in caps: MY FATHER. Without his bidding it the thought came, and he knew that he wanted to write of his father, paint his father, but could not, could not yet because he didn't know enough. It was the same as the fish, the loon, all of it. If he wanted to learn, to do, to write, to paint, to understand and know his father, he would have to see him, learn of him.

So. He put the notebook down and looked across the lake to where the flash of light had been. So. *So that's the way of it*, he thought—*if I can learn a fish, I can learn my father. So.*

So . . .

He stood and slapped the sand off his knees and bottom, put the notebook in the pack and rolled the boat over and pulled it to the water. A couple more minutes to get it around and aimed out and floating, and he jumped in and got the oars moving.

With sure, even strokes he drew a straight line across the lake from the island to the shore where his father still sat. Wil pushed the bow up on the grass and stopped.

His father's face was swollen from insect bites, and he had a pack with him, a sleeping bag, the binoculars, a few cans of pop, a windbreaker. *So sad*, Wil thought. *Why is this so sad? No, not sad, so . . . so rich. Why is this so rich? Almost too much to stand, what is here, this man who has been watching me, this man—my father.* "Hello."

"Hi." His father nodded.

"At first I thought it was that Weaver, but then I saw you through the camera lens."

"I know. I was watching you through the binoculars, and I saw you see me. . . ." He let it slide, smiling, a tired little smile. "We, your mother and I, sent Weaver off when he came back and told us nothing was wrong. . . . I wasn't spying on you, you know."

Wil said nothing.

"Oh, at first I maybe was spying. But after the newspaper thing came out and you told her all those things you didn't tell us . . ."

Wil shook his head. "No, wait. I didn't mean it like that. . . ."

His father smiled. "It doesn't matter. Really. We just didn't understand. And then when we read the article and saw the pictures, your mother and I talked it over and we decided that one of us should come and just take a look, just watch. We didn't know, you see. Didn't understand and maybe we still don't understand, but we thought if we watched you . . ."

He stopped because Wil had his hand up. "I wasn't trying to hurt you or cut you out or anything."

"I know that now."

"I was just sitting out there a bit ago, and I was going to write about something, and I couldn't because I didn't know enough . . ."

His father watched him, waiting.

". . . and I thought maybe if you wanted, you could come out there with me."

"To the island?"

Wil nodded. "Come out there, you know, with me."

His father looked away for a moment, across the lake at the island, then up at the sky. Then he sighed—a breath that came from all of him, the sigh—and looked back to Wil, and his eyes were shining. "I'd like that. Very much. If it's no bother. I'd like very much to come out to the island."

Wil nodded but said nothing. *There is so much here now*, he thought, pivoting the boat and helping his father get his pack in and settled in the bow. *There is so much here that I don't know, that I must learn, that is*

making my throat thick and making it so I cannot speak—
so much to write and paint and be that I cannot possibly
know it all.

And it came to him as he was rowing to the island,
his father sitting in the bow, looking across the water,
red-faced, swollen and red-eyed from what was between them, it came to Wil then, on the lake, as he
rowed toward the island how this would turn out, how
this would end. It was a high thought, a high and clean
and keening thought, as clear as the song the loon made
in the slash of moonlight that night on the lake.

It would end only when they found a bigger island.